Gregory Day is a novelist, poet and musician. His work has won the Australian Literature Society Gold Medal, the Elizabeth Jolley Short Story Prize and the Manly Artist Book Award. He lives in south-west Victoria, Australia.

Also by Gregory Day

A SAND ARCHIVE

GREGORY DAY

PICADOR
Pan Macmillan Australia

First published 2018 in Picador by Pan Macmillan Australia Pty Ltd
1 Market Street, Sydney, New South Wales, Australia, 2000

Cataloguing-in-Publication entry is available
from the National Library of Australia
http://catalogue.nla.gov.au

Typeset in 12.2/17 pt Garamond by Post Pre-Press Group, Brisbane
Printed by McPherson's Printing Group
Select French translations by Aurore Mulkens

Extracts from the following are reproduced
with permission from the publishers:
p.vii: Seamus Heaney, 'From the Canton of Expectation',
The Haw Lantern, Faber and Faber Ltd, 1987.
p.101: Helene Cixous, *First Days of the Year*, translated by
Catherine A.F. Macgillivray, the University of Minnesota Press.
Copyright 2008 by the Regents of the University of Minnesota.
pp.208–9: Courtesy of the artist and Roslyn Oxley9 Gallery, Sydney.
p.209: Bill McCormick, 'Sartre and Camus On Nature',
The Trumpeter, 13(1), 1996, http://trumpeter.athabascau.
ca/index.php/trumpet/article/view/275/1308

The author and the publisher have made every effort to contact copyright
holders for material used in this book. Any person or organisation
that may have been overlooked should contact the publisher.

This is a work of fiction. Characters, institutions and organisations
mentioned in this novel are either the product of the author's imagination
or, if real, used fictitiously without any intent to describe actual conduct.

The paper in this book is FSC® certified.
FSC® promotes environmentally responsible,
socially beneficial and economically viable
management of the world's forests.

for Jane Honman

What looks the strongest has outlived its term.
The future lies with what's affirmed from under.

Seamus Heaney

One

One

1

Change

Long before I ever met him I knew his name from the leaky desiccated type of a slim grey-brown volume, cheaply printed but essential to my research: *The Great Ocean Road: Dune Stabilisation and Other Engineering Difficulties* by FB Herschell.

When inspecting the boxes of his papers that were deposited in the university library later on, I came to know that the grainy photo on the cover of the volume was in fact taken by him in the early days, in 1966. He took quite a few other photographs at the time as well, mostly of hummock and shoulder, camber and heath. He certainly chose the most charismatic one for the cover of his book. Even so, it was hard to make out exactly what the image on the cover was depicting. In the background there was the forest-clad cove of Lorne across Louttit Bay. In the foreground a car tyre skid in deep sand. It was clear that at least one driver had had trouble getting through. With two men in overcoats standing not far from the skid it looked a little like a crime scene, which, in a subtle way, only made my urge to investigate the contents of the book even stronger.

So, the early world of the motor car, sand drift, the problems posed by dune shifts, roadmaking in the wind shadows. That gives you some idea of the spectrum. The poles of his range. Well, almost. This little book he wrote, the only one he ever published – and with no help from his boss Gibbon at the Country Roads Board, I might add – is so unassuming that you have to be seriously interested to notice what it actually contains.

What I was looking for when I first opened the book was narrative momentum. I had an idea that I wanted to write the largely untold history of the building of Victoria's Great Ocean Road in short historico-poetic vignettes, in the manner of the great Latin American writer Eduardo Galeano. I saw each hard-won detail of my research as the potential kernel for a historically accurate but dreamlike prose, an imaginative route back through time. And I soon had the sense that FB Herschell had been there before me.

Some of the other black-and-white photos the book contained were:

An old bridle track through a windy foredune.

The seaweed-dotted sand along the Eastern View beach.

Traxcavators on the cretaceous headland above the St George River.

The graphic vertical shadows of the slats of a 'Gascony palisade'.

A group of headscarved women planting in sand.

FB Herschell himself in the field, on the heath, amongst the controversial marram grass, his jacket flapping in the seeding wind, in tweeds and tie, in tam-o'-shanter, in deep Victoria. In 1970.

†

I was working at the bookshop in James Street, Geelong, when I met him. A long time after I'd finished my work on the history of the road. Like so much that went on in that bookshop, FB Herschell's presence came as a stimulating intersection between what is written on paper and what is actually breathing and alive. Suddenly those fusty initials on that slim grey-brown volume had become a living man standing in front of me, chatting with my fellow staff members. And rather than that leaky desiccated type on a dun background, his eyes gleamed with the freshness of ongoing life, his mouth constantly finding shapes of dry appreciation, his pleasure evident at finding other people who dwelt deep in the nourishing but often overlooked vanishing points of beauty and knowledge.

To be honest, though, the most important thing for me was this: he had liked one of the books I had written and in his understated way wanted to make that clear to me.

5

After the initial conversation, he'd drifted further into the shop, into the narrow space between European History and Modern Lit. I remember him standing there, like a swimmer gone into the waves. He had his back to History, scanning what we had of Proust. The usual translations, yes, and the first volume of the recent Prendergast edition, *Swann's Way* translated by Lydia Davis, but also the small book by Proust's maid, whose expertise was to read the sallow pouches under the writer's eyes like a diagnostic parchment, so that she could attend properly to the routines of his exquisite retrospection. There was also a volume called *The Book of Proust* on the shelves at that time, a blue-and-white hardback published in London in 1989, which surveyed the great writer from some stimulating and pithy angles. I had taken an interest in this book myself – it felt to me a bit like what Flaubert's characters Bouvard and Pécuchet might have written on Proust had they been invented after Proust rather than, through the stubborn linearity of time, before him. I'd always loved those two idiots from the last unfinished work of Flaubert. It being unfinished may have been partly why, but like so many great, and not so great, works of foreign literature, from Tolstoy right across to Enid Blyton, I had pictured all the action taking place in an Australian – or, to be more specific, a south-west Victorian – landscape. Thus, when Bouvard and Pécuchet sit on a Parisian bench and decide to move to the country with Bouvard's sudden inheritance, I have them sitting in my mind's eye on a bench in the Botanic Gardens in Geelong. And when they finally move to their country house to pursue their life-style fantasies I have them taking up their rural dwelling not in Normandy but in a house on Lardners Track on the Gellibrand River in the Otway Ranges.

Peering around a tall display vitrine and across the spines in our travel literature section I saw FB taking *The Book of Proust* down from the shelf. He would know it was a book originally ordered into Australia on indent, in the days before the internet. Whoever had ordered it had looked after it well, and as soon as it came into the shop we had covered it in clear mylar to keep it in good nick. I knew intuitively that its condition, as well as its content, would appeal to FB. Why wouldn't it? I felt sure also that some of the categories of interest marked out in the survey would capture his lively, polymathic mind. For instance, there was a *Dictionary of Places in À la recherche*, beginning with Balbec and ending in Vivonne. There was also a separate passage on Proust and music, which talked of Marcel and his mother playing piano together (a little like Jean-Paul Sartre and his mother) and how one of his relations, Louise Cruppi, introduced Russian music to Paris and was a friend of Fauré. It also talked of Proust's love for the organ music of César Franck, which I also enjoy. But the ingredient I suspected might appeal to FB the most was how Proust had discovered Debussy's *Pelléas et Mélisande* through the agency of a near-mystical contraption called a 'theatrophone'. This theatrophone was a telephone connected to a microphone in the Paris Opera which allowed the agoraphobic Proust to listen to a concert at home, a little like we might live stream a concert via the internet today. I hoped, as I watched the elderly bibliophile flicking through the pages, that he would find that anecdote and be stimulated by this convergence of technology and desire. But when he put it back on the shelf I felt sure he hadn't discovered it.

A good bookseller might then have made his way across and struck up a conversation, in order to swing things around to the subject. But I was never that, never a good bookseller in that way, and there was something about this unexpected entry into my life of the real man behind that inky name – *FB Herschell* – that had me far more concerned with letting any potential friendship form slowly rather than with selling him the book.

The Parisian theatrophone has always struck me as the kind of improvised ingenuity you find amongst people living by their wits in the outback. I marvel at that old geography-bound music being allowed to travel through the prehistory of a live stream. I crane an imaginary ear to hear what Proust heard: the scratchy, tinny notes from the Paris Opera clouded and fizzed by the thinness of the phone line and the microphone but nevertheless intact in each note's relationship with the other. The timbre would be more implied than anything else but the beauty would still be transmitted. The lack of sound fidelity would confirm that the process between the music composed and the listener experiencing it was as important as any reproduction of the originally played notes. How Proustian! Strange as it may seem, it was an experience like that for me just to have FB Herschell in the little shop. I could not quite believe the man behind the scratchily printed name was real and whole, and yet, like Debussy's opera for the Parisians in the seats of the auditorium that Proust could not bring himself to attend, there he was before me.

†

I should explain that back when I was doing my work on the history of the Great Ocean Road, useful published material was hard to find. It was not so much that there was a shortage of publications on the subject, it was just that they had nearly all been garbled by the often disingenuous impulses of tourism. Most of the material turned the heroic story of how the road was built by soldiers after the First World War into a trinket, a textual equivalent of a snow dome or a key ring, complete with commodified slouch hats and oversaturated vistas. As I read these publications I had the unsettling feeling that somehow the historical narrative of the returned diggers living in tents and hand-building the road in all weathers was being used only to get travellers to spend more money at the cafes. But the copy of *The Great Ocean Road: Dune Stabilisation and Other Engineering Difficulties* I had borrowed from the library was an exception. There was no schmaltz, no spin, only knowledge, technique, experience, and, every now and again, an unexpected glimmer of poetry.

At the time I was renting a weatherboard cottage in Lorne. Apparently the cottage was once used by the botanist Baron Ferdinand von Mueller, when he was down here on the coast collecting new plant specimens for his collection at the Royal Botanic Gardens in Melbourne. I worked with my laptop on the top of an old upright Waldmann piano, which I liked to think had been installed in the cottage before von Mueller's arrival and never removed. There was only a dial-up internet connection at the time that I was living there (this was in the year 2000), which allowed for much intermediary time waiting for relevant pages of my research to appear. Sometimes that would frustrate me, but more often than not I found the miracle of being able to receive such information without setting foot outside an old Otways weatherboard easily outweighed the frustration. These long waits also gave me time to think, to follow thoughts in a way I might not have otherwise, also to noodle and try out chords on the piano.

I had been given a CD of photographs of the soldiers building the road back in the 1920s and 30s by a kind man at a local historical society, and as I waited for various internet pages to appear I would open one or another of those images in Photoshop and begin to type lines on top of them. Some of these lines were triggered by small details buried amongst the material I'd found on the Ocean Road; others were just my own character imaginings from looking at the faces of the diggers as they swung their mattocks and pegged the route between, say, the S bends on the western end of that section of the road they nicknamed 'the Somme' and the incline past the now-popular surf break at Cathedral Rock. But one day, while I was looking at a scratchy image of the Devils Elbow – a hairpin bend that wraps around a dramatic point before curling onwards past the old tollgate at Grassy Creek on the way to Lorne – some lines of FB's from *The Great Ocean Road: Dune Stabilisation and Other Engineering Difficulties* popped into my mind. In the background of the image of the Devils Elbow was a wedge of ocean in greyscale, and it was as I was considering the similarities between the photographic flecks of the poorly printed image and the real-life gannets that wheel and soar past that very spot, that I recalled FB's lines:

Time passes, nothing stays still. Out there, in the ephemeral velocity of the high wind, what can be called a natural system? Likewise, in the transience of nature, what can be said to constitute a plan full of function? How, indeed, can we ever ascertain a real live measure?

Here, I realised, was an engineer-cum-historian reflecting on the essentially impossible nature of his craft. Or at least that's how it seemed to me. His questioning, his seeking through science and nature to approach more difficult and majestic truths than those materially available, seemed itself to come from the very space between those tiny photographic flecks and the 'real live' gannets that were their source.

I typed an abbreviated version of FB's words across the wedge of ocean in the image. Then I placed my foot on the sustain pedal of the piano, lowered my hands from the laptop keyboard to the ivory keys, and began to play.

The song the lines triggered was eventually called 'Theodolite', and by the time it was written and recorded many other songs had followed on its heels. My intended book had transformed into a musical project. And that, in no small part, was thanks to FB.

'Theodolite' had been ignited by something both present but also buried in his words. I felt that despite the pertinence of the questions he had asked in the passage, something else beneath the words, something untold, something as mysterious and invisible as the watery ocean world beside the road, had actually propagated the song.

Proust had written long ago: '*The essence of music is to awake in us the mysterious depths of our souls, which begin at the point where the finite, and all the arts that have a finite objective, ends, the point where science ends, and which one could call religious.*'

I felt sure there was something hidden, something almost religious even, in FB's words that resonated through his book and helped him speak of more than just engineering difficulties. I could not put my finger on it, but I knew that whatever it was that was buried there had given me better access to those 'mysterious depths of our soul'.

2

Slacks Between Ridges

DUNES IN THE DISTANCE. IN THE 1920S A MAN BY THE name of Lane had had the six-kilometre stretch of coastal road built from Point Roadknight, at the western edge of the present-day coastal settlement of Anglesea, to his Sunnymeade estate, on the eastern side of where I live here in the river valley at Split Point. Lane had had a car, and he wanted to drive it. On the other side of Split Point, where the upthrust of the Otway Ranges meets the coast to form the headlands of the Devils Elbow and Big Hill on the way to Lorne, returned World War I soldiers had begun work under the aegis of the Great Ocean Road Trust, carving a path into the hills above Bass Strait. Mr Lane's frustration was the roadless mix of dune and low cliff that ran the other way, east of where the soldiers' work had begun. If there were a road linking the dirt track that wound out from the rural port of Geelong as far as Anglesea to the point further along, where the soldiers' mattocks had begun to pierce the shore, then from his property he could drive to the east as well as to the west. There were already bridle tracks in the area – old horse paths that ran easily enough across the dunes and further into the Otways – and so the sight of the winding bridle track running along the coast from Point Roadknight towards his house at Sunnymeade became the kernel of his idea. Surely it was just a matter of widening it and firming it up?

Four decades after Mr Lane had his idea, FB Herschell stands in tweeds and waistcoat on that very ridge of dune, considering the problem. Somewhere between the dribble of limestone and sandstone rocks at Point Roadknight and the rising cliff of brick-red clay at Urquharts Bluff there has been another subsiding of the ground, and therefore of the road. An EH Holden with a boat on its roof has had a very close shave. It is the 1960s and the surf-loving holidaying traffic is, for the time being, increasing gently. What was once Mr Lane's private road is now the responsibility of the CRB, or Country Roads Board, and there is most definitely a problem.

FB stands beside a blowout of the dune. He looks east, all the way down the long moonah-green and cuttlebone-white littoral. Then west along it too, until the stern red brow of Urquharts Bluff stops the low foredunes in their tracks.

But the bluff doesn't stop the road. On the contrary. With the termination of the dunes and the rising, albeit temporarily, of the limestone cliffs, the road has a safe and stable base on which to travel.

It has been suggested to FB by his superiors that the dune is the problem. Putting a road amongst it has turned it from an ephemeral manifestation of nature into a site of possible danger. Just ask the couple of blokes who nearly met their maker in the EH Holden. If they had been killed in their fall, would they have been killed by a collapsing dune or a collapsing road?

FB considers the problem. There is a typical southerly wind on the beach, flinging sand at the land. He stands on the hummock by the road; below him it is low tide. He considers the action of the wind on the grains of sand on the beach and concludes that they are lifted from the beach, carried by the wind at a low altitude, until they collide with, and settle on, the dune.

A collapsing dune or a collapsing road? Was nature to blame, or culture? Which is at fault? In a single moment, a moment which will shape the rest of his life, FB Herschell becomes captivated by the question.

Half an hour later, standing on the beach below with Gibbon, his immediate supervisor at the CRB, FB is made to narrow his horizons. Gibbon has the data. In 1926 an early motorist (perhaps a friend of Mr Lane's?) broke the axle of his Buick on the subsiding roadway. In 1949 the road became impassable due to the formation of a dune slack, which induced slope failure in the limestone and left the unsealed road crumpled for sixty-eight yards.

In 1951 a hole the size of a large water tank appeared overnight and unannounced. The milk truck, which also carried the daily newspapers along with morning bread and coffee scrolls to the coast, only managed to brake before it tumbled into the cavity because a kangaroo hopping on the road up ahead had suddenly, inexplicably, disappeared. Then, in 1954, a Bailey bridge had been erected due to intense flooding. Further problems had occurred every couple of years or so until this latest incident with the EH Holden.

Half an hour later again Gibbon and FB stand just a few miles further along the road, on the western side of Split Point, where the road runs along the low duney shore through Eastern View before rising into the Otways. The problem here is the sand on the road. Slippery sand. Constantly scoured by the tides and the southerlies it is strewn over the road and presents an intermittent danger. Now, Gibbon announced, was the time to fix all these problems once and for all.

Listening to Gibbon's research being relayed in his husky cigarettey voice, FB felt the light pouring up out of the sea. He had read recently of an approach to music which decreed that if you wanted to understand sound you should study not the bell or hammers or strings of an instrument but the ear which hears what it plays. He had already spent hours, months, years, studying built structures: roads, bridges, all the physics of engineering pathways and crossings, in order to get his degree and a good position. But now, he realised with an instant swerve of relish, he was starting to think about what was under the roads, what perceived the roads, what came first; he was going to study the *ontology* of dunes.

†

Rising to the challenge, he decided to camp on site. This gave him an excuse to be on his own while workers wheel-barrowed the sand from the road at Eastern View and filled in the slip on Mr Lane's road with local gravel from the pits back towards the small farming settlement and railway siding at Moriac. The dynamic mix of dune and low cliff became a brindled thing at that spot. A smear of ochre interrupted the tints of limestone pink and sandy cuttlebone-white. It was like a carpenter thumbing putty into a cavity, except what surrounded the cavity would not necessarily hold.

He was away from his mother. Camping like the returned diggers who built the road running further along the coast. Breathing a sigh of relief.

For company he had the kangaroos and plovers. The gannets wheeling above porpoises out to sea. And Salisbury's *Downs and Dunes*. A bright grass-green, cloth-bound hardback. There had been next to nothing in the CRB library in Geelong, so with Gibbon's permission he had travelled to Melbourne and borrowed it from his old haunt, the Baillieu Library at the university.

His mother had both berated and mollycoddled him as he packed his tent and gear. That was no surprise. Gibbon too considered him decidedly odd for actually wanting to camp on site, but it was the weekend and he couldn't control him. If FB wanted to understand the situation better by boiling his billy there for a couple of days, then so be it.

For FB Herschell that brief time away from the floral-patterned bulk of his mother, camping alongside Mr Lane's old road with only the thrumming of his tent flap in the wind to bother him, made for an unusually enjoyable situation. There was the dune, the complexities of the brindled hole in the road, his diary, the explanatory paragraphs and diagrams of Salisbury's book, and the sun and moon going about their business in the autumn sky above the sea and shore. It was – atmospherically, personally, *intellectually* – perfect. Bliss.

But he said his prayers. Yes. And he sized up the constellations. His brain had got him this far, got him to the point where Gibbon had singled him out, almost daring him with the task 'of saving lives'. This gave him confidence, of course, but nevertheless he filled the dark space between the constellations with Our Fathers for the saving of his own soul. He would be missing mass on Sunday morning. He prayed for himself, for his father's eternal rest, and for his mother's back pain to cease in time for her solo game on the Monday night.

He listened also to what he called in his diary '*the*

unconditional love of Mary in the waves'. The way it came in a moonlured rumble, crashing softly in its frequencies against the tight resistance of the ground, displacing stubborn ledges, stiffened banks, wedges of sand, opening, freeing, clearing. Exposing sharp roots too. He had never before strung a line in his mind between Jesus's mother and his own but now he did. His own mother made him feel both safe and insecure, volatile, scrambling about between judgement and the search for some small cleft of approval. He would be assembling bits of coloured paper on a board in one room and feel her eyes watching him from the next, so that his hand hovered, hesitated, a scissored hemisphere of an orange dune in his fingers. Or he was in the little scullery kitchen, where there was never any light. He climbs the blackwood stool to watch his mother bake. She wears a brown apron over a grey frock, and he wears a brown jumper, knitted for him by Aunt Lyn from Forrest, above grey shorts. He watches as she puts the ingredients into the heavy pink ceramic bowl: butter, flour and sugar, with a measuring jug of milk ready off to one side. She is baking the cakes for the wake of his father the next day. Then something occurs to her, she seems to get a fright. She goes to say 'Blast!' but refrains, and, telling him to keep a close eye on the ingredients (in case someone steals them?), says she'll be back in a minute. He hears her possum-hustle in the hallway, hears the back screen door slam. It's the washing, he thinks, as simultaneously he registers the dabs and pitter-pats and pings of

19

rain on the iron roof. The washing will be mainly overalls, his dead father's body hanging upside down, and frocks, her living frocks, plus his school shorts and shirts, and their underwear. He wishes it could be otherwise. He wishes his dad had not slumped beneath the machine bench at Fords; he wishes the ingredients in the cake bowl could be otherwise too. While she's gone he kneels on the stool and wonders why those four things – butter, milk, flour and sugar – always made a cake. A brown cake. The potential of the ingredients in his mind is endless. The ingredients of the world. He peers over the bevelled lip of the bowl and his tongue slips out the side of his mouth in concentration. He puts his hands in, feels the butter weight, the way it sticks to his palm but is greasy at the same time. He watches the flour fall. The sugar is white soil, the milk white water. If these four things can be squished about to make cake, then what else can they make? How about a model train track?

When his mother returns, she finds the bowl sitting neatly to one side, its ingredients spread over the bench. Three-quarters of the butter has already been rolled into definite lines, the flour is grouped in small triangular piles of freight, the sugar spread flat in a white field between them.

She does not notice the orderliness of the arrangement; sees only a mess. He is cuffed off the stool, gruffed to the bathroom to wash his hands, lectured to about waste.

For the rest of the morning he sits on his bed in disgrace. He'd been surprised by how stubborn the ingredients had turned out to be; he expected them to transform more easily. But he'd kept at it, as the rain grew heavier on the roof, and he became lost in creation. Now in his room, he is fingering a football card. Carlton. Centre half-back. Bert Deacon. He smiles to himself as he imagines Deacon lining up not at centre half-back but at full forward, on a wing – or, even better, wearing the priest's collar and vestments the next day as they all say farewell to his dad in the church.

All that anxiety was not a part of these white waves tumbling towards him in the dawn. That anxiety was more like a hurtling train of fear. He was in a carriage of cold stitched-leather seats. Yet he was nowhere; it was all in his imagination, of course. On the canvas stool beside the breezy tent on Mr Lane's 'long beach road' he was as still as a hawk on a hillside. He remembered how when the Colemans came, the cousins on his mother's side, all that anxiety had somehow *mobilised*. His dream's wide gauge – so rare, so inventive, so expensive – had narrowed back to the size of sausages and scones, narrowed to the pecking order at Cheetham Salts, narrowed to thin smiles with thin bakelite lips. Morris Coleman, Uncle Morrie, had no lips at all. Nothing to run on, just duty, small-town approbation, Pivotonian crumbs.

The violin was taken down from the top of the bookcase in the hall. The big dark shelves almost to the ceiling. He was not yet tall enough to reach the violin case up there so his mother did it. She was taller than his father, who, if he had not died, probably wouldn't have been there to help anyway. His dad had avoided the Coleman cousins like brussels sprouts. He had always been doing overtime.

And do you think the Colemans were interested? They were looking out the window, through the leadlight, out through the referred frown of the eaves to the bare street. As if they longed for that bareness. Where no-one was feeling anything. As the strings of young Francis's violin began to resonate, the bareness was cultivated like vines by a vintner, a vintage bareness following the protocols of the vines. Bad habits were reinforced daily, as his mother so often said.

He played 'Waltzing Matilda' in the front room. Such a show from a boy so young. As he played he tried to think only of the notes. Tried to stop seeing things. Though the bank of the billabong was sandy, though there was a slug travelling across the bark of a fallen log, though the flames of the fire under the blackened billy had orange tips, he averted his eyes. Thought of the notes. As the Colemans looked out at the street.

With a different audience, he realised, lying back in his tent in the dune, perhaps he might have dived, not into the billabong but into the billy itself. With a different set of relations, he could quite possibly have drowned in what he was cooking up. Or he could have cooked them all up in the music. He would have been freed then, to play in the waves, with Mary, whose love moved even the heavy sand.

†

In the dunes by Mr Lane's road that night FB Herschell actually had two books with him. One was Salisbury's *Downs and Dunes*, the other by Charles Baudelaire. I know this because he recorded it in his diary. Of *Downs and Dunes* he said nothing at this stage, but of Baudelaire he wrote down one single quote, and then a thought of his own about the dune, which, with the hindsight of history, seems to follow.

> *Yesterday on the crowded boulevard, I felt myself jostled by a mysterious Being whom I have always longed to know, and although I had never seen him before, I recognised him at once.*

FB put the lines through the two *hims*.
Below this he wrote:

> *I wonder what happened to the kangaroo who disappeared down the hole in the road in 1951. Gibbon didn't say, but whatever the case its fate was both the fault of the dune and no fault of the dune at all. Is this possible? I wonder what the milk truck driver thought?*

†

We had our regular polymath customers in those days when I worked at the bookshop, but more often than not the polymaths were the quiet ones whom it was hard to get to know. The customers who spoke a lot, who went on and on about the size of their libraries and their love of books, generally turned out, when pressed, to be a bit of a let-down. With the shyness of polymaths, however, there were no shortcuts and you wouldn't ever know the extent of their knowledge or the depths of their reflection until, purchase by purchase, you began to piece it together over the years. FB would turn up with that quiet twinkle in his eye, but never with that much to say. It was as if he presumed that we at the shop understood from personal experience that the rock Sisyphus pushed to the top of the mountain, only to watch it roll to the bottom again and again, was actually a book. It was not the same book every time, but nevertheless it was always a book. He'd pushed Proust up the hill, and Orwell, Musil, Cervantes, Dante, Isambard Kingdom Brunel, Simone Weil, Braudel, Thomas Telford, Duras and Sarraute. There were so many different types of rock, from so many different periods, and from so many different sections of the shop. History, transport, poetry, drama, mythology, architecture, music, religion, philosophy. After his death, I had the chance to look through a portion of his library and was amazed by the detailed history of his voluminous overseas book ordering that I found between the pages of each volume. Our local bookshop was just that, his local, but FB Herschell shopped far and wide.

For example, a 'picking slip' from an unknown source, typed out on a white sheet of paper folded to fit inside the pages. Dated 29 November 1995 it read:

This picking slip was produced when we received your order. It may have been manually adjusted during the picking process. S/O next to a title means we have sold out of that title.

It seems that on this occasion FB's strike rate had been good. There were no S/Os on the brief list.

1/417
Mr FB Herschell
33 Milipi Ave
Geelong Vic 3220
AUSTRALIA

77	1	Foster, SE	*Colonial Improver*	7.95
105	1	Steegmuller, Francis	*A Woman, a Man, and Two Kingdoms: The Story of Madame d'Epinay and Abbe Galiani*	14.95
435	1	French, Marilyn	*The Book as World: James Joyce's Ulysses*	9.95
500	1	Seidel, Michael	*Epic Geography: James Joyce's Ulysses*	12.95
	4			45.80
			Freight	10.00
				55.80

There was also this one:

Invoice: Statement Fuller d'Arch Smith Ltd
30 Baker St London W1M 2D5
Tel. 01–722–0063
Invoice No. 224802
5. Nov. 80

To   Francis Herschell
           33 Milipi Avenue

Geelong Victoria 3220
Australia

Thomas Telford, Engineer   9.00
                                Postage .70
                                Total £9.70

Or this:

Editions A et J Picard
L'Oblat, Huysmans JK

. . . and countless others.

✝

Apart from his visits to the bookshop I only ever had two or three conversations of any length with FB, and one of those took place in the bakery-cafe just up from the shop. By that stage the area around James Street was becoming fashionable, but for many years – in fact, for the whole long life of the bookshop up until then – this part of Geelong was dotted with empty, unleased properties. It turned out that FB Herschell had an encyclopaedic knowledge of the city and its history and knew all about the evolution of the James Street area.

We happened to be walking out from amongst the books and onto the street together – me headed for my lunch break at the cafe, he headed I know not where after his hour of browsing – when I made a casual remark about the possible pros and cons of the encroaching gentrification.

The old man smiled knowingly – not as if to say, 'I've seen this kind of thing attempted here before,' but, it seemed to me, with an understanding of the essential innocence of human endeavours, how they come and go, rise and fall, like so much sand on the wind. And then, having smiled so wryly, FB suggested, with a hint perhaps of the lifelong public servant, that the coming change would be a good thing for the town, for its inhabitants, and particularly for the people who liked not to have to travel through to Melbourne to get their fix of good culture or coffee. In the tail of this reference of having to go to Melbourne for culture an ironic look crept into his eyes.

Five minutes later – I can't remember which of us suggested it – we were sitting down together at the end of the large old wool-classing table in the cafe on James Street for lunch.

Despite the vast difference in our age, as we ordered our sandwiches I remember being acutely conscious of the similarity between us. I could spend weeks, months, a whole decade with people my own age and have nothing to say whatsoever, but here, with this man a good forty years older than myself, I knew I could talk, and listen, for hours.

But hours it was not to be; instead, just one hour, due to the parameters of my lunch break. As we'd already begun talking on the street about gentrification and change, and because it was implicit in our writings – and, specifically, those of each other's writings that each of us had read – that we both had thought quite a lot about these things, no preamble or scene-setting seemed necessary. There was no need to establish common ground. We talked on the subject as if we had been having such a conversation for years.

I had a sense that day of FB as not only stimulating and friendly but as a man wherein a wide universe of reading had been digested and then applied to the intimate details and textures of a local region. To a certain extent I suppose I was still confusing the book with its author, the publication with the man, which could explain why it took me by surprise when he began to recount, as a particularly interesting example of gentrification, a story not about Geelong or the Great Ocean Road, not even about Melbourne or even Australia, but about a little-known island in the Seine, the Île Seguin.

As our sandwiches were delivered FB began to tell me how the English artist JMW Turner had made a sketch of this D-shaped Parisian island in the early 1800s, when it was connected to both the Sèvres and Boulogne-Billancourt banks of the Seine by charming wooden bridges. FB explained how back then Sèvres and Boulogne-Billancourt were villages in their own right, though they were now suburbs of Paris. At the time Turner sketched it the island was owned by an industrialist and was used as a large-scale tanning factory. The industrialist's name was Seguin, hence the island's name. After the First World War the island was bought from Seguin by a man named Louis Renault, who had prospered during the war and already ran automobile factories on both the Sèvres and

Boulogne-Billancourt banks. Through the tumultuous decades of the twentieth century, Renault's factory on the Île Seguin grew to become the largest in Europe. Its buildings covered nearly every square metre of the island and by the 1960s some ten thousand workers would cross the now-concrete bridges from either bank in first light to clock on for their day's work.

Eventually, however – and this was the pertinent point about gentrification that had triggered FB's recounting – Renault built other, more modern factories on sites in the French and Spanish countryside and the pre-automation equipment of the Île Seguin factory became obsolete. The factory eventually ceased operations and a huge and expensive clean-up of the asbestos buildings and the contaminated soil got underway. The architect Jean Nouvel, after fighting unsuccessfully to have the factory buildings preserved as a cultural heritage site, finally proposed to turn the island into an eco-arts hub. The D-shape site of Seguin's tannery and Louis Renault's toxic but iconic factory was now to become, FB told me, an island of concert halls, studios, galleries and exhibition spaces. There would also be a grand indoor garden, enclosed in glass, and the entire complex was tipped to become a home for media and entertainment companies.

Perhaps, as I had when reading his book on the Great Ocean Road, I sensed something in FB's Parisian anecdote that drew me in further. I know this myself as a writer: if you give up all the information too quickly, the reader becomes bored and has no reason to keep turning the pages. Likewise, there was something in the way FB told the story of Île Seguin that had me leaning in closer and closer, leaving my sandwich untouched. Was it the look in his eyes when he ever so briefly mentioned the factory's significance in the momentous demonstrations of 1968? Was it his faraway look as he recounted one historical stage of the story being buried by the next? Or was it nothing so concrete or visible but, rather, something that had been absorbed into his being and therefore into his telling, a charged undercurrent of his experience?

In truth, I didn't have the equipment – intuitive, intellectual or otherwise – to understand the mysterious energy that was acting upon me. All I knew was that after we'd paid the bill and said our farewells I went back to the shop in a very different mood.

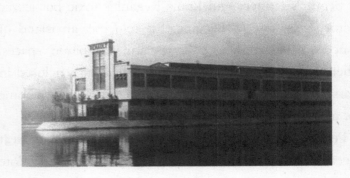

†

There is certainly a way in which I can see Mr Lane's building of his 'long beach road' as the start of a gentrification process which continues today along our home coast. Except Mr Lane, of course, unlike the twenty-first-century construction companies undertaking the renovation of Île Seguin, didn't have to clean up decades of asbestos to get his road underway. CJ Lane was – to use that rather loaded English term – a gentleman, and there was nothing at all *gentrified* about the kangaroo that disappeared down the hole and saved the life of the milk-truck driver back in 1951. Lane's road could not, as yet, be completely divorced from the decidedly ungentrified environment around it. And this is the challenge still for so many contemporary Bouvards and Pécuchets hell-bent on experiencing the health- and life-affirming properties of the sea. The French environmental historian Alain Corbin describes the discovery of the sea's allure amongst the industrial middle classes of the eighteenth and nineteenth centuries as reflecting a view of the sea as both '*the enchantment of the watery mirror and the source of profound certainty*'. But, as the kangaroo found out in 1951, there was no 'profound certainty' about a road being built beside a powerful ocean, or if there was it could only be achieved through a temporal illusion akin to that created by the sea itself, or Corbin's 'watery mirror'. In truth, a littoral environment is a realm of such fluency that the solidities and illusions of ocean and shore can never be successfully divided. Right here on the seam, in the briny domain where kangaroos are known to wet their club-like tails in the surf, every animal would already have understood that. Until, that is, Mr Lane decided to build his road.

†

The one other significant conversation I had with FB happened closer to home – here, in the yard of my mother's house in Split Point. Unbeknown to me he had a great friend called Anna Neilson, whose house sits only a small distance from my mother's, behind two impressive ficifolia trees on the bank of the river. I knew Anna from the thereabouts – a tall stately woman slowly walking her dog in the dusk. I had often noticed too a stylish vintage car parked on the verge beside her house and garden, but had never put two and two together. Having had lunch with FB in the cafe in Geelong, however, I was now more alert to the convergences, and not long after that lunch I bumped into the two of them walking along the riverbank with Anna's dog.

Behind them as we met I could see the Renault Ondine parked on the grassy verge. The penny dropped. That of course was FB's car, the two of them were companions. Not even a minute had passed in our friendly conversation before, having summed all this up, I began to relish the prospect of having more to do with them both in the future.

Only a couple of days later, while working away in the sunroom of my mother's house, I heard voices in the yard outside. I looked up to see FB and Anna Nielson coming along the driveway.

We had an amiable chat, though interspersed with tentative pauses and somewhat nervous silences. FB had mentioned to me over lunch at the cafe that he was finally putting together a record of the technical and historical articles he had written for local publications over the years. Leaving aside his one book, *The Great Ocean Road: Dune Stabilisation and Other Engineering Difficulties*, the list ran to quite a number of pages and the task of compiling it would have taken quite a bit of time. When he mentioned the daunting task to me in the cafe I had encouraged him to continue, and now he and Anna were dropping by to give me a copy of the end result.

From what I now know in retrospect, and from what I have gleaned from fishing through the archive of all his professional papers, personal journals and diaries which were deposited at the university after his death, and from what I have also gathered from talking to other people who knew him, and from piecing together my own reflections from the memories of our few brief meetings before his death, I realise now that such a personal visit from FB Herschell was rare. The idea, also, that he would come around to 'show off', as it were, his own accomplishments, was almost completely out of character. Perhaps if I'd lived in Geelong like him he would have rung first. Perhaps it was only because we were here in the more relaxed atmosphere of the small coastal town that it felt easier for him to just drop by unannounced. Whatever the case, I now realise that, given FB's shyness, the feeling I had of being honoured by this unexpected turn of events was well founded. In truth, I didn't know the half of it.

The visit didn't last long. I didn't even have a chance to offer them both a cup of tea. Standing there on the small terrace leading off the sunroom, FB produced a document from the folds of his jacket. I took only a cursory glance at its pages before expressing my admiration at the list of works. Anna made some jokes about having to use a crowbar to get FB to come by and drop it off. After all, she said, what was the point of going to all the trouble of compiling the bibliography if you weren't going to make people aware of its existence? Well yes, that's right, I agreed emphatically.

FB stood by, smiling sheepishly. Despite his years his face still contained the impish energy of a boy. I could sense his discomfort at his achievements becoming momentarily the centre of attention, but I was also in no doubt as to the powerful sense he had of himself. He gave off the feeling, which I also have, that although we may go to endless amounts of trouble with our passions and work, and although we become proud of our accomplishments and consider them useful, in the end none of it really matters. Everything – the mind, the heart, the roads, buildings and bridges, the music, the libraries and the bookshops, not to mention the books themselves – will all be washed away in the end. Our rock will simply roll back to the bottom of the hill.

Nonetheless we speak, write, build, pave, compose. We go on, as Samuel Beckett would say. We go on. This was a phlegmatic truth that the man who came around to my mother's house that day well understood. It was in fact a downright existential truth that helped make his quiet life worth living.

FB and Anna Neilson's visit was so brief that the sunroom door was opened but never closed, the tea never made. But after I had walked them out to the gate I went back into the sunroom and stood with his document in my hands. The FB Herschell bibliography came in the form of a thin stapled booklet, printed on high-quality paper and, in keeping with FB's 'light under a bushel' approach to his own achievements, it was not called a bibliography but a 'checklist'. A humble checklist.

The booklet, however, ran to twenty-five full pages. It included all FB's articles published in local publications between 1959 and 2010. I noticed on the first facing page that it had been 'typed by Anna Nielson'.

†

During this period I was only ever working at the bookshop in Geelong two days a week. The rest of the time I was at home writing. Three months after FB and Anna's visit, while walking from where I parked my car at Kardinia Park football ground to the bookshop in James Street, I bumped into Anna Neilson again, this time at the intersection of Myers and Gheringhap streets. I was standing in the median strip waiting to cross over and continue down the slope past the mossy slates of St Giles and on to the shop, when the lights changed and she pulled up in her car.

We were surprised to see each other outside the gentle context of Split Point, me standing there in the middle of the raw grid of Geelong streets, she firmly on a mission behind the wheel of the car. We managed to have a brief conversation before the lights changed again.

It was a rainy day; I didn't have my umbrella up but Anna's windscreen wipers were on and she wound down her window to speak.

She was on her way to the hospital to see FB she said, with a regretful but nevertheless warm smile. Is he sick? I asked, surprised. She winced. Yes, she said, nodding. He's dying.

The lights would change again quickly and she would have to continue on her way. We both knew it was not the place for further discussion. But anyway, I didn't know what to say, it came as such a shock.

Of course I had no reason to expect to have been notified about his condition, but nevertheless Anna reacted as if apologetic. Did she think FB himself would have told me? Did she think I'd heard it on some local grapevine? Didn't the whole world know, after all, that FB Herschell, the man who drove the vintage French car around Geelong and the surrounding coast; the man who would quote Hélène Cixous in the original to the seagulls on the shore at the end of Moorabool Street – *avec une suele larme on peut pleurer le monde* – the man who as a grief-stricken boy contemplated diving into the swagman's billy while playing 'Waltzing Matilda' on the violin for his cousins, didn't the whole world know he was dying?

It seemed not. Through the car window I could see Anna looked momentarily confused. And then the lights did change, she winced again, we waved, and her eyes turned to the road ahead. The hospital was only two blocks further along. She was nearly there. Nothing, after all, is that far from anything else in a city the size of Geelong.

†

It is hard in the internet era for people to comprehend the lag that used to exist between the emergence of new cultural trends in Europe or America and their arrival here in Australia. For instance, people speak of the counterculture of the 1960s as a global phenomenon that transformed the world from the prim materialism of the postwar era to the open-house experimentation associated with Andy Warhol, Wilhelm Reich and the Beatles. But in Australia the '60s actually happened in the 1970s, and in some ways it was only our direct involvement in the Vietnam War that saved us from missing the cultural revolution altogether.

One can easily imagine then, as FB camped on the long beach road between Anglesea and the Split Point cliffs in 1966, that the days of CJ Lane and the building of his private road some forty years before in the 1920s would have seemed far more local and familiar than Warhol's pop art or the cover of *Sgt. Pepper's Lonely Hearts Club Band*.

The conversation of an anachronistic era, the delay in the cultural current, was everywhere set fast around the young CRB engineer. And no-one represented it better than Gibbon, his immediate supervisor.

As FB's fascination with the enigmas of sand – its changeability, its slow and granular accumulation, its propensity to shift and slump whilst all the while growing heavier, deeper and higher – began to evolve, rather than support him in his new train of research, Gibbon attempted to block FB at every turn. At best his encouragement was grudging.

When FB reported to Gibbon's office after his ruminations on the problems of the long beach road and at Eastern View, he found Gibbon with his face to the light of the window over McKillop Street, smoking his pipe. If Gibbon had been able to peer into the leather satchel FB had placed on his desk, he would have found, alongside Salisbury's *Downs and Dunes*, Baudelaire's journals and FB's notes on the problems of the road, a small slender hardback copy of Rimbaud's *Poems of the Damned*, translated by Jacques Le Clercq and published by the Peter Pauper Press in New York, with illustrations by Stanley Wyatt. Since he'd returned from camping out on the long beach road FB had had this handy pocket edition tucked safely away in the interior pocket of his Harris tweed. He wore it close to his heart, even as he attempted to intuit the hydrological memory of the dunes and the pros and cons of introducing marram grass to stabilise the sand.

> *On the slope of the hill angels twirl their*
> *woolen robes in grasslands of steel and of*
> *emerald. Meadows of flames leap up to the*
> *crown of the hillock. On the left the leaf-mold*
> *of the ridge is trampled underfoot by all the*
> *murderers and battles that ever were, and here*
> *all disastrous tumults describe their appointed*
> *curves.*

Gibbon squeaked a blue cumulus of burning shag out the corner of his mouth and made sure to paste a cast of authority over his countenance as he turned his face back into the room.

'So,' he intoned. 'What do you think now that you've boiled your billy on the problem stretch?'

'I think the dunes will never be still,' was young Francis Herschell's reply.

Gibbon cupped the pipe in his hand. Breathed out his nose. 'That's not news,' he said.

It wasn't. What was news, however, was that Gibbon had three shaving cuts on his asbestos-grey jaw, each emitting a virulent anger into the room. The cuts were in an isosceles shape, FB noted, the Euler line of which was livid.

'We're actually looking at two very different situations,' FB offered. 'One quite clearly involves a problem with the mobilisation of sand but the other may well be a problem that the sand itself can fix. And given all the miles of coast-line that fall within our remit, on the Bellarine, even the bay, I'd like to do some more general study on the subject.'

Gibbon grimaced. 'You are not here, Herschell, to tell me what you'd "like to do"; you're here to tell me how we're gonna fix the road. Any clues?'

Gibbon's 'gonna', his slight tip towards the vernacular, was evidence that he was already, within a minute of FB's coming through his office door, in the vicinity of his personal boiling point. FB understood that these 'gonnas' and 'wannas' only surfaced at the extremes of his boss's moods: either happy, as in 'you wanna go to the pub?' or, more often, angry, as in 'we're gonna fix the road'. On this occasion, FB was surprised he hadn't thrown in a 'bloody' for good measure.

'I'd like to investigate the potential of marram grass.'

'I see. To what end?'

'To stabilise the dunes.'

'Grass, you say.'

'Yes, grass. But not just any grass. *Ammophila arenaria*. Marram grass.'

40

Gibbon leant back in his chair. He actually chuckled sarcastically. 'Yes, well, I'm better on tarmac, macadam, bitumen, you know. Grass is a little out of my ken, shall we say.'

FB was instantly bored by this reaction. Intriguingly, he noted in his diary that he felt 'a very familiar native creature roll up inside me'. He nearly shut his eyes and began to curl up along with it, but instead fixed his gaze on Gibbon's livid shaving mishaps. He hoped that that might annoy him further. Get him excitable as a way of saving FB from sleep.

'So,' Gibbon puffed into the silence.

FB kept his eyes on the isosceles of cuts. 'I think if we want durable solutions out there,' he began, 'short of building another Bailey bridge, we could do worse than to investigate marram grass.'

He'd only mentioned the Bailey bridge in jest but as soon as he had he regretted it. The Bailey bridge had been developed during the war as a portable lightweight means of crossing otherwise impassable ravines, and Gibbon's whole world had been shaped by the war.

'Mmm,' Gibbon said, placing the pipe back between his lips. 'We could have done with a couple more of those Baileys up in Moresby. For the time being at least it's gotta be more effective than grass.'

There, FB thought. From angry to happy in twenty seconds. The 'gotta' was proof.

He hated the way Gibbon's ignorance kept governing

these situations. It was as if somehow, by using the comparison, FB was proposing they build a bridge out of grass.

He shook his head. 'No,' he said. 'I wouldn't think so.'

'You wouldn't think so. Is that right?'

'It is. Grass in this instance could hold the dunes into a more permanent shape, a little like a skeleton. It could alleviate the drift problem at Eastern View and, by building up the dunes, protect the low cliffs on the long beach road from being so exposed to wearaway and weather.'

'Sounds unlikely. A proven piece of engineering on the other hand . . .'

'Yes, it's obvious.'

'I'm sorry, Herschell?'

'It's obvious. By that I mean it's *visible*, the bridge, it's there for all to see. Problem solved. Complainants placated. Whereas the grass would act more in harmony with the conditions – like a skeleton, as I say.'

FB stared again at the three shaving cuts.

'A grass skeleton, you say?'

'Well, yes. But that's only one analogy. Another is to think of it as a reinforcement. As in a concrete slab. A firm foundation to match the surrounding stone.'

Gibbon's face took on a querulous cast. FB wondered if he was confused. Shifting his gaze to look into his superior's eyes, he saw stains in the whites, tobacco, cloudy. The dullness of those eyes confirmed the absurdity of the prospect. A huge great eyesore bolted onto Mr Lane's beautiful long beach road. FB groaned internally. It was not necessarily a case of a single problematic culvert; it could well be a case of ongoing and unpredictable camber. It felt like a big mistake to have introduced the bridge into the equation at all.

'Well then,' Gibbon concluded, puffing hands-free again on the pipe and tidying up his papers. 'Plenty to consider then. Perhaps I'll get Warren to look into the costings of a Bailey bridge, as well as some barrier work at Eastern View.'

According to FB's diary Keith Warren was a local optician. He was also the Barrabool Shire treasurer. He had fought with Gibbon in Northern Africa during the war. So FB demurred, rather bitterly. There was no getting round the old veterans club. He left the office, without even leaving his notes for Gibbon to peruse.

3

Velocities

THE ANSWER TO WHY FB HAD DECIDED TO CAMP OUT ON the long beach road was the same as why he began to spend both days of all his other weekends going back and forth to the big Melbourne libraries on the train.

The entry for 'Mary' in the sixteenth edition of *A Catholic Dictionary* – published by Routledge and Kegan Paul from Broadway House in London in 1960, and revised throughout by members of the staff of St John's Seminary, Wonersh – runs to many pages. It follows on from the entry for 'Martyrology' and is followed by the entry for 'Mass'. This book has a blood-red dust jacket, behind which are bluey-green boards. The lettering on the dust jacket is white. On the endpaper at the front of the book FB has written something in blue ink and then rubbed it out emphatically in the same. That is most unusual to see in any of his books – it is the single instance of such a defacing – yet some of the letters he has scribbled over are still distinguishable.

What he has written runs to four short lines. I can make out the word 'Above', which is the last word of the first line, but nothing else until the last line where I think it says 'S.W-S.S.W.' as in 'South-West – South-South-West.'

So, *'Above'*, and then *'S.W. – S.S.W.'* Why on earth he would have made the rare gesture of furiously penning over this script is mysterious, as it does not seem to constitute either a confession or a blasphemy. One possibility is that his mother did it for him. The rubbing out. But why would she? Would scrawling meteorological marginalia into a Catholic dictionary be sufficiently blasphemous that she would further deface the pages with such messy rubbing-out? It wasn't even a Bible, after all. All I can think of is this. Perhaps, having endured the early death of her husband and then the precocious development of her quite brilliant son, she wanted him to change his shape no more. To hold him back. To *stabilise* him, preferably through piety. It seems, though, that he had an irresistible longing to swim out through the waves. To look back at himself from within the meteorological coordinates of unconditional love.

†

And so he nut-nut-nutted it out. First of all, the ambitiousness, even the folly, of building a road in a dune

environment, and then the potential aesthetic and func-
tional beauty of it. If it could be made sound.

Truth was, in a semi-diagrammatic representation
to scale of the root system of marram grass he saw a
future. The way its venous roots delved, the grass itself
only a small part of the plant, secured by hidden things,
fastening fingers, splaying and plummeting through the
vertical dune. There was not enough information in the
libraries, though, and what there was was not necessarily
applicable to an Australian situation. He did read that
in the early days of the colony *Ammophila arenaria* had
been trialled at Port Fairy. But what would be the point
of planting the wrong type, and finding it to be as super-
fluous as Gibbon's Bailey bridge? And what of hydraulics,
transpiration, pore space, dune travel and form? Dunes
were like all scientific problems: they moved. Just when
you thought you had the parameters defined, they shifted.
Like time. Water. He also read how on the Atlantic
seaboard of France a movement of *'about 30ft a year has been
observed with local advances of up to 80ft'*. This sentence struck
him like a tide. A massive movement. He felt something
likewise shift inside him.

✝

The night before he travelled to see the chief engineer at
Port Fairy he sat over tea with his mother, pretending to
listen. She reached across the table, put her hand on his,

when she realised he wasn't. He sprung back into the field of her tenderness, as pliable as a pomaderris strand to the shape of her needs.

She fought with what he knew, the way he dressed himself up before he left the house in the morning: the houndstooth suit, the Surrey tie, the brogues and hat. No-one else they knew dressed like that. No son of anyone she knew went so far in his presentation as that. FB would go on the train to Melbourne – studying, he said – and come back with a loud bag from Buckley's department store or whatnot. She'd let him in on her distress, she'd bother him, or after the fact tell him how difficult he made things for her. Like that one day when, as she was coming through the streets of Geelong, down the Moorabool Street hill towards the bay, and happened to see him crossing the street, most likely on his lunch hour, it had occurred to her that he looked *notorious*. Like someone from *another family*. Or someone whose dress betrayed *no family* at all! The image had stuck. The son she dreamt of most nights, the son she shared the house with, the son who liked mash and sesame snaps, strolled through the sea-and-wool town like a stranger. Normally she might have quickened her step to catch him up. But that time on Moorabool she stopped, turned aslant, back into the crowning southerly. Hoping he wouldn't see her. She wouldn't have known what to say.

'Promise me you'll not miss mass down there,' she is saying now, in the smell of lamb fat and peas, tightening her grip on his hand where it rests beside the butter dish.

He smiles at her. 'Of course not, Mum. I'll bring you a written report.'

His facetiousness is comforting to her. But she pulls a stern face. 'You would not be at work in the church, Francis. One cannot "report" and "pray" at the same time.'

'No,' he says, frowning. 'You're quite right. So I'll report back on what I see in the hotel in the evening. As a way of keeping myself out of the mischief.'

She rolled droll eyes, took her hand off his, content now that she had regained his attention.

He continued to smile, naturally happy to have pleased her.

But there would be no such report from the Stump Hotel in Port Fairy. In his diary entries for the visit of July 1966, which was conducted chiefly to inspect the reported success of pioneering marram grass plantings on the dunes between the town and the volcanic crater of Tower Hill, he notes how empty the hotel is every night, how boring the barman, how 'rugged' the food. He reads James Clarence Mangan, Behan's *Confession of an Irish Rebel*, and a crisp book by a young poet from the north, Seamus Heaney. All Irish fare, in keeping with the pub's atmosphere. It is the title of the young poet's book that has most attracted him. *Death of a Naturalist*. In his research he has discovered that Port Fairy used to be called Belfast, a long time ago, before the marram grass was planted to save the town from sand and before the squelchy native pastures were drained dry by nostalgia.

†

FB imagined those 'local advances of up to 80ft' in France were not trifling things and an unexpected conversation on the golf links at Port Fairy confirmed the fact. Despite his tweeds he could not much play golf, knew not a mashie from a niblick, but enjoyed occasional success with a seven-iron. On the eighth green on the Tuesday of his visit, in the vicinity of the dune hummock which he and his two playing partners – Pat Considine, the chief engineer of Moyne Shire, and his golf-mad wife Noreen – had been discussing throughout the round, FB mentioned these shifting dunes of France in relation to the local movement (much less significant since the marram grass) of the dunes as outlined by Considine.

'That fits,' Noreen Considine remarked, as she employed the plumb-bob method to line up her putt. FB had already noted in his diary how taken he was by the chief engineer's wife's interest in her husband's work. She had much to offer, it seems, as they made their way around the course in unusually pleasant winter weather, and now, with a better memory for details than her husband, she recalled as she stood over her putt how, in the course of Pat's investigations into the dune problem for the farmers of the district, he had discovered that the mecca for the study and research of such things – i.e. sand dunes – was indeed in France. Paris, France.

Noreen holed her putt, the sound of the gutta-percha rattling around in the ceramic dish was music to her ears. She beamed, FB noted.

Then, on the short walk to the ninth tee, Pat Considine offered this sage advice: 'Yairs, well, what Nor says does ring a bell. I remember this much: there's bugger-all work been done on the subject in Australia. But that's why you're down here, isn't it, Herschell? What we've done here in the Moyne is ground-breaking.'

'If you'll excuse his pun,' said Noreen, before teeing off in her tight, yet well-fitting, clothes. Having holed the putt, it was her honour.

†

An aside. Noreen Considine most likely would have been considerably older than FB, who himself was in his mid-twenties at the time, but I do sense in his scribbled entries for 12 July 1966 the hint of an attraction. A little reminiscent of the proportions of visible to hidden sections of the marram grass physiognomy FB was in Port Fairy to study, I have the feeling that the anecdote of how Noreen Considine came to inform FB that France – indeed Paris, France – was the world leader in sand dune research was merely, if you like, the green strand above the rhizome. One thing at least is certain:

Noreen Considine could have had no idea how significant that small piece of information she gave FB would turn out to be.

†

Visiting the dying is invariably an awful business, but sometimes not visiting the dying can be worse. One day, on a break from my writing, I was walking alone by the river near home when a friend of mine, who teaches art in Geelong, told me the news. It was approximately three weeks after my conversation with Anna Nielson at the intersection of Myers and Gheringhap. I didn't know Francis Herschell well; I had no reason to be so upset. But I was.

Perhaps sensing my distress, my friend left me to walk on my own by the river. As soon as he was gone I felt the strangest sensation. I saw in my mind a white luminescence, in something like the shape of a lizard's tail, tapering off and voiding the very air as I walked through it. It was as if a creature-shaped vacuum was continually opening up behind me as I moved.

To shake this sensation off I went and sat on an old sawn-off pine tree stump. The river, narrow, with reeds, was brown. The luminescent lizard tail disappeared as I sat down. And then a sentence from the French novelist Nathalie Sarraute came into my thoughts:

Those who live in a world of human beings can only retrace their steps.

I did not ask myself why those mysterious words of Sarraute's had come to me like that. The spontaneous appearance of phrases I have read in books is something I am used to. Nevertheless, I must have read those words, what, maybe three years before? As I sat on the pine stump it was as if the silent brownness of the river had closed up the strangely luminous vacuum and replaced it with the liquid facticity and cadence of words.

Those who live in a world of human beings can only retrace their steps.

I started to retrace my steps. Why had I not gone to visit the old man in the hospital as I intended? I had been busy, sure, but not like a prime minister. I had been frightened, yes, but is that what had stopped me going to see him? I doubted it. Perhaps I felt deep down that it wasn't appropriate, he being so private, he and Anna Neilson too, and that I would have been intruding? And yet Anna's smile at the intersection of Myers and Gheringhap streets was so warm that it made me feel almost as if I could be part of their inner circle. The inner circle of his dying.

This feeling, I believe now, was because of what FB and I shared, even as we were only getting to know each other. Perhaps for my generation in Australia it has been easier to live the examined life, easier at least to find friends who would be excited by Proust's theatrophone, or Marguerite Duras's honesty, or the creative experiments of Georges Perec and *Ouvroir de littérature potentielle* (Oulipo). But when FB was young, especially in Geelong, that wasn't such an easy task. His penchant for aesthetic engineering, for roads, bridges, aqueducts and the solving of structural problems, was solid stuff that could be easily understood and explained, talked about at the pub, at the nineteenth hole, in the grandstand of the football ground. But Malraux, Camus, Baudelaire and de Beauvoir, Sartre, Piper, Betjeman, Claude Simon and James Joyce, Sylvia Beach and Barbara Hepworth, Francis Webb and JB Priestley, Grazia Deledda, Primo and Carlo Levi, Gwen Harwood and Paul Celan, Apollinaire and Gide and Flaubert and Radiguet and Pagnol and Julien Gracq . . . all these names that I have seen on his shelves and amongst the notes, diaries and journals of his archive, the sound of their words, their phrases and rhythms and insights, had to be carried around alone, almost like one's own most private thoughts. Perhaps, at a pinch, he could have explained his British influences: John Piper designed the stained glass for Coventry Cathedral, after all, bomb-ravaged Coventry Cathedral, which almost made him a *digger*; and Betjeman was the Queen's poet, the laureate, so he was a Commonwealth *edifice*, a Menzies man of sorts; then there was the Irish bent: the Wilde and Yeats, the AE and Flann O'Brien – well we were all half Irish, weren't we? But the French stuff, the experimentation, the *art for art's sake*, that was harder to explain. If FB had've pricked the surface of Pat Considine's opinions he would have discovered a quiet but nevertheless unmistakable *disappointment* that the repository for the study of sand

54

dunes was in France. They were a weak, mincing, effeminate and cowardly lot, the French. The war had proven it. Gibbon of the CRB would have concurred. Capitulated to the Nazis, they did, handed over the keys to Notre-Dame without blinking. Deserters, collaborators, thieves, not to be trusted. Their only claim to fame was pastry, or, at a push, *style*, but wasn't *style* how you behaved in a crisis? In the end, when it had really mattered, they had proven they had no style. Just lopsided hats and long breadsticks.

Such views persist, though like so much these days they sit as repressed ballast in Australia's prosperous ship. On deck we move about freely, take in the scenery, the music, the madeleines and the Armagnac. We can agree openly, even in a *pub*, with Jean Baudrillard when he says that the whole arc of western culture was geared to arrive at a moment when all our material desires – clothing, architecture, sex, art, cinema, cuisine, travel, sport, education – would be satisfied, and that we reached that moment some years ago but did not realise it, so that now we are merely continuing in the automatic pursuit of the very things we already have. In FB's prime years though, in the years when he was beginning to think about sand, theories such as that were only spoken of in enclaves that he did not frequent. And anyway, it was not so easy for him to insert such things into conversation with so many other *thoughts-interests-ingredients* swirling around like grains of sand in his head. Would they settle one day? Would the gales stop and allow his thoughts to take a simple form and outline? Would those thoughts then become the internal hummock that quells the wild sea? He didn't know, but in truth he may have doubted it, at least for as long as he lived with his mum and she *needed* him. And so he lived on, reading, thinking, accumulating, questing if not in his body then through his interests, far, far from the single-fronted house in Milipi Avenue where he and his mother did the nightly crossword.

Whatever the case, he and I connected. At that late stage in his life, and in the haven of the bookshop in James Street, there was a compact. If Oulipo was mentioned, or a topic as licentious or outrageous as Wilhelm Reich and his orgone accumulator, no-one blinked an eyelid. Some laughter might be heard, born of the nonchalance of those who'd arrived on earth too late to really understand the strictures and crises of the twentieth century and the experimentation they produced, but nonetheless in the bookshop, FB, who did understand such things, felt less alone. We connected. Not through the disembodied glitches of the internet but with all our five senses working. In the same room as each other. In a room in a regional city, a room full of books in Geelong.

But then he was dead. Just as we were about to get going. Just as I was about to tell him about the theatrophone, and to ask him what he thought of *Charlie Hebdo*, of Christopher Barnett, of Houellebecq's *Submission*, of Macron, and of Modiano. Now I was left alone on the raw stump of postcolonial pine, with the brown, brown river.

The words of Sarraute filled the vacuum.

Those who live in a world of human beings can only retrace their steps.

After I don't know how long I got up and retraced my steps – literally this time – back to my house. As I went the bright vacuum, the luminous void-shape of his passing, re-emerged, flicking occasionally, a lizard's tail of light behind me. I entered the house, sat down at the table with his presence all around me, took up the checklist he and Anna had dropped off, and, once again, began reading.

Two

4

Slip Face

IT HAD BEEN FIRST WRITTEN IN A SMALL BLACK-AND-RED notebook, alongside metro routes, timetables, and *'cabbage, fish, marmalade'*. Then it had been scored with chalk on a wall in the Sorbonne. Now it was written in dark grey under-paint on the apartment building opposite the cafe, below two ghastly griffins of the Second Empire.

The forest precedes man,
The desert follows him.

The mist had come with the first light, but as the buildings and the earth below them were warmed it soon disappeared from Rue Monge. Mathilde and Georges had been up all night yet their conversation did not lack for energy. They sat at a corner table by the shining window, looking out onto the day's first cars making their way along the street. Mathilde, the young woman with freckles and red hair, was cursing.

'You are talking about something that was new six decades ago. Have you not heard of Kupka?'

'Yes, well I have. But this is not linear. This is about unrealised realities.'

réalités non réalisées

She scoffed, scornful, her face flung back as if towards Gascony. 'It is no such thing,' she said. 'It is about unrealities.'

irréalités

'No, it is a question of vision,' Georges replied. As he argued with Mathilde he was not cross so much as certain. He spoke for a time about Kupka. About *The Yellow Scale* and how there would be no Beatles without it. No *Sgt. Pepper's*. He spoke of how it was for Kupka when he was living not in Prague or Vienna but in the Parisian suburb of Puteaux. Thus Georges enumerated the nodes of his knowledge of the Czech abstractionist.

'But the Puteaux Group was also called the Golden Section!' Mathilde cried, aghast. 'Their very name was a materialist thing.'

chose matérialiste

She went on. 'It is the difference in length between your arm and your leg, between the leaf and the stem. It is not an abstraction! It cannot be spectacularised! It must retain its real context to be available for eternity. Otherwise it is like a gold that will refract, the structure will slump, the surface will fray: into ugliness, and violence.'

Georges raised his hands into the air. He was exasperated now. 'And so,' he retorted, 'do we just go on, with
ancient harmony in our minds, like a patrimony? Like a
warehouse full of Papa's grain?'

This struck a nerve in her. The red-haired, freckled
Mathilde. The foot traffic was increasing outside. People
with sleepless hair, smoking, touching. Stepping over
rubble, piles of cobbles, bent steel, prone street signs
and other refuse on the street. She rose from the table
brusquely, pointing through the door.

There, across three days and nights of detritus, of
rumpled crowbarred boulevards, was the scrawled phrase
on the wall that had ignited their conversation.

La fôret précède l'homme,
  le désert le suit.

†

After farewelling Georges by Aux Assassins, she arrived
at the gallery before midday, still not having slept, but
somehow refreshed now that she was alone. She had
invited him to join her, to demonstrate her point about
Kupka, but he was tired. She was glad. And anyway, she
needed time, and was sure that history would make her
point for her. When all the crazy ideas in the air became
granular again, before taking their place back down on
earth.

Unbuttoning her cardigan, she crossed into the second, smaller room, and saw she would not be alone. A thin, neat middle-aged man and a younger man with an English coat and a *mouche*, not saying much. Two elderly women, one with *Le Figaro* spread before her, the other speaking quietly but rapidly, as if to the wall.

She would at least be able then, she thought, to properly *see* the dunes.

pour voir les dunes

The two men discussed the paintings in an intermittent way, quietly, so that even as she shared the space with them she could only make out fragments of what they said. She gathered, however, that the older man had brought the younger man to see only the Mondrians, and specifically the dunes. Perhaps he too was not from Paris – his accent sounded like that of her father's friend René Pernac, who was from the Médoc. Whatever the case, the older man did not stay long and left quite suddenly, as if a duty had been accomplished, an introduction performed.

She stood then with only the younger man's quietude – she felt a shyness surrounding him, perhaps a lack of confidence, even as he absorbed himself in the paintings – and the two older ladies viewing the adjacent wall.

pour voir les dunes

Her fingers rested on the cold key to her apartment in her cardigan pocket. With no-one looking she adjusted her bra. She began to insert herself into the gaps between the dabbings of paint, let herself enter the swales, lean on the slopes, feel the sand. Then, just as emphatically, she returned to the image, the paint that made the image. She didn't think of Zeeland, where the paintings had come about, nor of the dunes where she had been made. But she had needed to come there nevertheless. She had quoted the line to Georges – *'Art is dead, but the student is a necrophiliac'* – not five minutes before they parted ways at Aux Assassins, he to sleep before rejoining the throng on Boulevard Saint-Michel, she, guiltily, to stand aloof before the Mondrians.

The old woman with *Le Figaro* began to quote news from the reports. Perhaps these ladies owned the gallery, Mathilde thought. Or perhaps their sons or daughters did. It was hardly a normal place for recitations of the news.

She cringed as she listened to the breathless hatchet-journalism. But the facts themselves were actually enthralling, tyrannical statistics which could only be estimates anyway.

On the Île Seguin . . .

At the Sorbonne . . .

In Lyon . . .

The old woman's tone was excited, not so much approving as entertained. Her friend must have been listening but she appeared not to be, staring as she was at the annotations beside the compositions on the otherwise white wall.

Mathilde took her time, her breathing beginning to slow after hours of chaotic activity and urgent thought.

The outlines of sand began to crystallise in front of her and she compared their rhythm to the cadence of the old woman's recitations. Eventually the other, more self-absorbed of the two women said, *'Assez!'* and immediately the dunes lost their chintz, the room fell silent, but for the sound of the newsreader folding away the newspaper.

And so they stood, the four of them, before the paintings in the Galerie Sarcon. Until the young man sporting the *mouche* under his lip and the English coat turned and left the gallery, with a leather tread that echoed from the walls.

She thought the impeccable old ladies would go now that the paper had been folded but no, now they began to talk properly, about the events of the night. She'd had enough. They'd made no mention of what she'd seen, where she'd been; they may as well have been discussing their cats.

She caught a last glimpse of his coat, his tan-coloured coat, as she turned her face away from the ladies' dialogue.

'They commandeered a bulldozer from a construction site and began to move things into place for barricades.'

'They levered the street sign on the corner of Saint-Michel and Saint-Germain and began to wield it like a flag.'

'It would have been heavy.'

'Yes, but there were so many of them.'

She followed him out onto Rue des Quatre-Vents. He was not hard to follow, his stride was long but slow; for a time she was content just to keep him in her sights, past the bus stop, past the man with an embroidered F on his black jacket, past the snickering pigeons, until she felt like a sleuth.

She caught up with him under the plane trees at Saint-Sulpice. A green line of life in the city, still untouched except for one whose trunk had been chopped through overnight. The tree lay askance, a toppled monument, a green queen fallen, as if in supplication before the church. On the short stub of its trunk a black telephone sat, like a creature from Magritte. Immediately she imagined picking up the receiver and dialling home. To give her papa an account of what had happened, to tell him how at 2 am the CRS had charged, tear gas exploding into the once joyous, now caustic air.

Instead she motioned to the thin young man standing under the nearby tree, which had not been cut down. She pointed at the telephone on the stump. He smiled at her. It was not a smile with laughter in it, more a smile of someone simply glad to be known.

She knew he had noticed her in the Galerie Sarcon. That they had considered the same paintings: the dunes made iridescent, but still loyal to the sources of their form.

'Je suis Cézanne du Louvres,' she said.

He frowned.

'Shall we make a call?' she said then, in English, but he still frowned.

Slowly his smile returned.

'Cézanne wanted to burn the Louvre,' he said eventually.

'*Exactement.* We could dial in a progress report.' Again she looked at the phone on the sawn-off stump.

It was the tree, he realised later, that had given the telephone its metaphysical powers. The feeling unthinking tree. Suddenly, after a night such as that, with the old world jemmied loose, the phone on the tree had a direct line to the most intimate sources of the world.

Yes, let's ring Cézanne, she had said. The thin young man in the well-made tan coat was right: Cézanne did want to burn the Louvre. The old master from Aix had come into her mind unbidden, like a sea urchin floating to the surface of blue water. But why him? Why not Frantz Fanon, why not a prank call to the politicians, to Guy Mollet?

The thin young man set her right. Proposed the obvious. 'Why not Mondrian?' he said. 'Why shouldn't we call him instead? We could call him to come back and play with us on the dunes.'

She had smiled. Felt a peace in the hollow. And couldn't quite believe her ears.

5

Grains

T HAT WAS THE SATURDAY, 12 MAY, AND, ACCORDING TO
FB's diaries, no-one in the city, on either side of
the many arguments, the many lucidities and irrepress-
ibilities, was quite sure. The police had attacked at 2 am,
and were now, in the daylight, dismantling the barricades
that had been heaped up through the previous day and
overnight.

They introduced themselves. To each other, and to
history. Mathilde, Francis. Francis, Mathilde. Both in
support of the momentum taking place since the government had closed down the Nanterre campus earlier in the
month, but both from a long way away: Arcachon, Geelong.
Gascony, Australia.

They stood for a time, joking about the plane tree
telephone, deciding in the end, yes, to call not František
Kupka or Paul Cézanne but Mondrian. The phone had

rung out. They had put this imaginary lack of success down to intellect. Not theirs but his. He was not taking calls from nature anymore. He was too busy with the arrangement of his grids.

Later, in the Café Peretz, while Mathilde was in the toilet, he sat alone and amazed. The telephone in fact was their communicating angel. They had not needed to make a call to any painter, any anti-colonial freedom fighter such as Fanon, or any politician-devil like Mollet. It was as if the phone on the plane tree stump had blithely connected them.

Or that's how he felt.

They had just begun talking.

As if in mid-conversation.

†

The weather was warm, the light threading the dishevelled streets almost mystically, reflecting the underlying limestone, sandstone, gypsum and chalk. When she suggested he take off his coat, FB realised the expensive coat was excessive, almost stupid. He enjoyed clothes, and had felt that the coat was at a Parisian pitch, but now his embarrassment showed. You must be hot? she'd asked rhetorically, but he didn't like the shirt he had on underneath, let alone his own body. Yet she cajoled him into it. She told him that the tone of the coat, its interesting discolorations, reminded her of the miles of marshes, called *les landes*, inboard from her childhood home at Arcachon on the Atlantic coast. 'It is an abstraction,' she said, laughing now, with this playful reference to Mondrian.

'I am a dune buried in a coat,' he had said.

He could see how she enjoyed that stroke of repartee, which relaxed his doubts about his shirt at least, bought for $5.80 at Eddy Elias Menswear in Geelong; a grey synthetic short-sleeved business shirt, with some anonymous monogram fraying badly on the chest pocket. He had meant to buy three French shirts as soon as he arrived but had felt too self-conscious and could not summon the courage to deal with the grace and confidence of Parisian shop assistants.

'*La dune enveloppe les landes.*'

She tried this follow-up joke on him but with no success. So she explained. 'The dune dressed up in the marshes,' she said, and told him of the marsh-farmers who had walked for centuries on stilts across the so-called 'useless' squelchy lands of which his coat was a simulacrum.

He assumed a mock innocence. Enlisted, and not for the first time since he'd been in the city, an implied antipodean innocence. Any resemblance was unwitting, he cried, but she reassured him, told him how much she loved *les landes*, or what was left of them.

'Last night the streets were like *les landes*,' she said. 'Finally we were on stilts. Unproductive to capital. Beautiful.'

He saw in his mind then a horizon of tussocks, tumbled

upon one another and forming a barricade the same colour as his coat. The barricades Mathilde had helped to build were not made of tussocks but of anything that could be found close to hand, objects of the city converted, decolonised. And though the streets were not literally moors they were also being recycled, composted, diverted from their official function.

He understood her. He couldn't believe it, but he did. It felt natural to him. Even the hidden fervour he sensed hovering around their duet was something he could understand. Something that had sat in the pit of his excitable stomach since he was a boy.

Yes, he understood. He could hardly believe he had slept all night, all his life in fact, not now that he had met her properly.

†

They walked away, through detritus, clusters of spectators assessing the drama, Mathilde leading them away from the trouble. At Saint-Germain-des-Prés there were meetings, also outside the School of Mines, but miraculously as they came through Montparnasse towards the Porte de Châtillon she saw no-one she knew, no-one to wonder why she was walking in the opposite direction.

As they walked he began to tell her why he was in Paris. That he was a civil engineer studying sand dunes. The older man she had seen with him at the gallery was his professor. The professor had alerted him to the Mondrians.

†

They walked and walked, eventually towards the *périphérique*, through Châtillon towards Clamart. She told him later that she thought they were seeking nature, as if it could still be found on the edge of the city, as both a consonance and consort. Could the meter man with the bad cough across the street putting a ticket on a green Morris feel the same way? Perhaps. Could the girl with the short braids wolfing down a baba? Maybe one day, in the circadian calendar of her heart.

A lady carrying a long pole passed them, heading back in towards the action. Two nuns, and a man wearing a surgical collar. All with faces set, headed for the aftermath of the barricades. An apple-green 2CV. A blue car, a yellow one, two blue 2CVs. He had recorded it all. He wrote down, too, how she had described helping to lift such cars overnight, hauling them up onto their sides in the Rue Gay-Lussac.

And now a single file of scouts passed them on the other side of the road. As if to confirm all arcane regimentation.

Mathilde and Francis walked, *drifted*, the other way.

†

To rebel against the rebellion. Is that what they were doing for those few short hours? Was this a pastorale, were they drifting, or actively resisting the moment, resisting history?

At the corner of Rue Pasteur and Avenue Augustin Dumont, where the clouds gathered, she offered him her hand as they began to cross the road. His breath was nearly taken away by the touch. Suddenly, though, the house in Geelong, in Milipi Avenue, the house to which he would presumably return, filled the spaces of his mind. With its own spaces. His bedroom, its single bed, the built-in bookshelves, the windows looking onto the grey paling fence, the dark alcove in the kitchen for the stove, the back porch, even the matrix of its flimsy trellis, the screen door whose handle you had to lift up rather than down. He even saw the lonely birdbath in the backyard – lonely because he saw clearly, at the heart of this most sensuous moment, how it was empty of water. In his absence. He'd done well in his studies of the French language because, like a trained parrot, he had a talent for rote learning. So now he said: 'The birds. Where are the birds?'

Les oiseaux. Où sont les oiseaux?

It was a fey question, in the middle of the city there, with all the major union and factional affiliations readying themselves for a major public collaboration, the meetings going on with lively debate and impassioned declamations of protocols and their deconstructions. She knew this and yet the question had a charm. She imagined his homeland as a vast lilac aviary, against which Paris seemed a blank page, its famous details erased by the emptiness of its skies.

The sky was white now. She was looking up and the sky was white. It had been the blue of the season but now, looking up, the clouds had gathered. The sky was white with no birds.

'Where are the birds?' she said in English, as they arrived on the far side of the Mairie de Clamart. Then, in the window of a *tabac*, she saw an orange canary in a cage. Letting go of his hand suddenly she rushed over. The *tabac* was empty. No-one behind the counter and a single Monoprix bag on the counter. She moved straight to the cage. She leant through the silver light of the window, her arms aglow, and unhooked the cage door. The orange canary titled its head at her quizzically. And then, smiling broadly through the window at FB, she came out of the *tabac* again.

La porte a été ouverte, mais l'oiseau va-t-il s'envoler?

'The door has been opened,' she said, taking his hand once more. 'But will the bird fly?'

†

Later that day, after the blandishments of Clamart, the words appeared on the walls of the city along with all the others. From the moment of the first student demonstrations at the Nanterre campus, indeed from February to

April in Chicago, Brussels and Munich, the student revolution had become a pageant of scrawled one-liners, the architecture of the city the pages of an artist's book.

VITE!
(quick)
IL EST INTERDIT D'INTERDIRE
(It is forbidden to forbid)
LE BONHEUR EST UNE IDÉE NEUVE
(Happiness is a new idea)
NE ME LIBÉREZ PAS, JE M'EN CHARGE
(Don't liberate me, I'll do it myself)
SOYEZ RÉALISTES, DEMANDEZ L'IMPOSSIBLE
(Be realistic, demand the impossible)

They had found brown paint in a tin strewn the night before. They rushed to buy a brush but could find nothing open. Then Mathilde had seen one also lying on the ground, amongst the refuse of a barricade.

On an apartment building at 26 Rue de Buci, between Saint-Germain and the Seine, they wrote the words in large block type, the brown paint slightly discoloured by the blue paint that had not quite dried on the brush that they found.

LA PORTE A ÉTÉ OUVERTE, MAIS L'OISEAU
VA-T-IL S'ENVOLER?

6

'"Back to the Land"
Is the Schtick of Pétainists'

IN A RESTAURANT THAT NIGHT IN MONTMARTRE HE HAD
made the mistake of telling Mathilde he could hardly
believe she had grown up at the very place on the south-
west coast that he was about to visit on a research trip.

She had raised her shoulders and shaken her head. 'But
you can't leave at this moment. It would be like running
away from history.'

He explained that he had no choice, that a field trip with
his professor had been organised as part of his studies.
They were to leave for Arcachon and the Dune du Pyla
in two days time. He admitted then that he was looking
forward to it.

Implied in his comment was a dangerous nostalgia,
Mathilde explained. She said she could sense him already
luxuriating in an impending peace.

And then she said: '"Back to the land" is the schtick of Pétainists.'

At first he didn't know what she was talking about. Marshal Pétain had headed the collaborating French government under the German occupation, he knew that. But sometimes, even despite his ability to retain vast amounts of information, and despite his aptitude for French studies, he too easily confused the subtle vowel sounds of the language he was hearing. Thus, in this instance, as they dined on sole and drank white wine on the far right knoll of the city, he had heard *pédéraste* instead of *Pétainist*. Or, rather, he had not known exactly what he had heard but *pédéraste* was the closest approximation.

He did not know what this issue of 'back to the land' had to do with him, let alone with the molestation of children. But, intellectually ambitious as he was, he tried. Perhaps it had something to do with a destructive romanticism of innocence, of natural purity. The Nazis had had strong notions of a golden earth, after all, an impossible earth, and look at what they did to children. But how was the pleasure of his anticipation of leaving Paris in two days time for the *Grande Dune* and the landscape of her childhood in any way abusive?

Eventually he decided to be brave. 'I don't understand you,' he admitted.

She stared at him, frowning intensely.

'But then again,' he said with a smile, 'we've only just met.'

He intended this last comment as a charming joke but she didn't seem amused.

'You are suffering from *distraction*,' she said.

He noted that she used the word as if it was a disease, like syphilis, or the flu.

'Do you think so?'

'Yes,' she said. Then, with less certainty, 'and it seems it's contagious.'

In the corner of the restaurant a young man played flamenco guitar. Every now and again he would get up and move around the room, soliciting coins with an upturned black velvet hat. He now stood beside Francis and Mathilde. FB reached instinctively for the wallet in the inner pocket of his marsh-coloured coat, but she waved the guitarist away. '*Plus tard*,' she said.

The guitarist kept moving amongst the tables. The room was dimly lit; if it wasn't for the glow of a fish tank high on the wall above the door they would hardly have been able to see the musician when he sat back down on his low chair, replaced his hat, and took up his guitar.

There was a bright orange-and-green-striped fish in the tank and now, for the first time since they had entered the restaurant, it caught FB's eye. As if the mere mention of the affliction *distraction* had produced such an exotic temptation out of thin air.

He quickly corrected his gaze, looked back at Mathilde.

'And so, the dunes in the Galerie Sarcon, the Mondrians,' he ventured, 'are they a distraction too?'

She thought for a time, or pretended to.

'No,' she said. 'They are *les arts décoratifs*. My studies. But they can be temporarily put aside for more important things.'

'Like what?'

She smiled. 'Like letting birds out of their cages.'

He grimaced then, remembering the flush of her skin as they had written the words on the Rue de Buci.

'But you would have my cage closed?' he said.

'No, no,' she exclaimed. '*Voler! Voler!* Go ahead and fly. But fly in Paris. Where the air needs you.'

†

On the Sunday he woke late, knowing the Galerie Sarcon would be shut. Mathilde had kissed him on both cheeks on the street outside the restaurant before saying goodbye. But it was not the touch of her lips on his skin that had the effect. It was earlier, when they had finished their meal and she was describing to him, by way of demonstrating her point about distraction, the life she had led as a girl on the Gascony coast. Loosened now by the wine she was confessing how she fought to keep her nostalgia for it at bay when, in enunciating the word *pinasse*, a tiny jewel-shaped bead of her saliva flew illumined through the dimly lit air and landed directly in his open mouth.

Mathilde did not seem to notice what had occurred. She continued apace, describing the freedom she'd had as a tomboy fishing from her *pinasse*, a small rowboat made

80

from the local pines that had been planted across *les landes* to drain the marshes. But it was as she talked that the young FB had grown more properly *distracted*. He sat, nodding his head, but barely paying attention at all.

He had closed his mouth as soon as he felt the wetness land. The arc of that single bead of her saliva was instantaneously etched onto his brain. It set up a tingling in his whole being. The ease with which it flew, the perfected shape of its trajectory, the softness and scintillation of its touch as it landed. He sat silently, convinced he had a pearl sitting on his tongue.

He went to bed that night, after riding the bus from Montmartre to Jussieu, still savouring that moment and the sense it gave him of having been penetrated by Mathilde. In the morning, when he woke, the sense he had of the pearl of her on his tongue was still clear. The nature of their interconnection could not have been sweeter. He had taken her into himself, into his mouth and his bloodstream, not in a sloppy ungated kissing way but with a perfect economy and singularity.

Yes, that was it. The singularity. That single pearl. It was only one drop, one drop of her, and it was all that was needed to alter him forever.

†

Mathilde spent that Sunday in a state of confusion. Back in the cafe with Georges and two friends of his from

Nantes, she didn't breathe a word. She listened as they debated what should happen in the coming days. A general strike for Monday had been called on Saturday after the extent of the police violence towards the students on the night of the barricades became evident. Three of the main union alliances – the CGT, the CFDT and the FO – had announced a joint demonstration and forum for the Monday morning. The plan was for students to show their solidarity with workers by showing up first thing at the Renault factory on the Île Seguin, then leaving together for a mass demonstration which would start from the Place de la République in the afternoon. Georges was worried about the fragmentations that would ensue, arguing that Stalinists, communists and socialists of every stamp would attempt to colonise the moment. His friend Andre assured him in good humour that such political encrustations were so irrelevant nowadays as to be subjects for anthropologists. Nevertheless, said Gilles, who was Georges' oldest friend, a thousand fights will ensue and blood does not flow in museums. These were the streets, after all.

Gilles was keen on Mathilde but as they sat drinking beer at the table she was doubly oblivious. Why, she asked herself, had she talked for over an hour in the restaurant of the night before about things, such as her *pinasse*, that did not really exist anymore? Memories were the internal museums of those who lived in fear of change. She did not like to think of herself as such as person. The *pinasse*, as it moved amongst the shoals and currents of her child-hood waters, had a dexterity she wanted to employ in her life in Paris now. It was not a symbol of some sweet yet distant perfection, yet as she had spoken of it to FB she had felt her sighs rising like fish under her voice. As if the very ocean was a nostalgia pouring its tides through the mouth of the Bassin d'Arcachon, and pouring too like an invisible dye through the bloodstream of her present life. But no, the ocean was a fact, a wedge of blue she held in the corner of her mind. The resinous air, the cries of the gulls, these were not things she longed for, not fairy tale histories to which she longed to escape; they were facts, that's all, facts like limbs, hair, organs. Facts of her.

So why then had those fish-sighs risen, just when Paris was being overturned?

As a bus full of Japanese tourists went by she snapped out of her reverie. A man passed by the window of the cafe eating a cake. The question remained unanswered.

7

Wind Shadows

Î LE SEGUIN. ON MONDAY MORNING THE TEMPO THAT HAD been building at the Renault factory finally reached a crescendo. He was there. Roaring across the bridge with the tide and the fervour. In the air he sensed both the old grievances of the Marxist working class and the new insouciance of the student rebellion. Beneath the pouring crowd on the bridge, the river itself was flowing with irony. It seemed to smile at him as he looked downstream; it seemed to be winking in the spring sunlight.

The weather was beautiful. He kept his feet, used the flats of his hands to balance against the shirts, the coats, the shoulders and sleeves around him. How, they had all been wondering, would the students and the workers get on?

It seemed the Renault plant covered nearly every last inch of the island. Once FB had stepped off the bridge he saw how a voice through a megaphone was marshalling the river of bodies. He passed with the throng – excitable, joking, intent – into a vast factory shed with a ceiling almost as high as the sky. On either side he could see the stations and equipment of the assembly lines. Enormous steel presses and cylinders, flat-gridded bays, painted workstations with lathes plastered over with colour photos cut from magazines of talismanic sunshine, holidays, sex. Here and there workers were at their stations, refusing to be distracted, going about their tasks as if nothing out of the ordinary was happening, as if chassis would be assembled as on any other day.

Instinctively he felt a concern for these hermetic, stubborn souls. Alone in the city of light he related to the dignity of their solitude, and thought of his father. But abuse was being hurled at these chassis-monks manning their steel altars. They were told to stop fantasising through their glued pictures of countryside and girls, to get out with the rest of the crowd, to actually *live* the sunshine and sex.

The faces of the solitaries remained inscrutable, their overalls like soutanes pressed clean. The blue Gitanes smoke swirled.

The crowd came to a standstill at the shed's far end. Conversations flowed, necks were craned towards a central point: a speaking dais on a hoist, metres in the air.

First the CGT representative spoke. It was just after 8 am. For too long de Gaulle's machinery had been gummed stuck, but to close down the universities and attack students was 'the last refuge of scoundrels'. (The CGT representative used the English phrase for this.) A rare moment had arrived, where the light had converged. It must be seized. On this island in the city, where a heartless regime had been created within a beautiful world, hidden systems were now being clarified and exposed. The minds and bodies of Paris were aligned. *En masse*.

FB could not see the speaker's face, only hear the sharp, emphatic, nasal voice. The response was strong, even with the factions. The FO, the Trotskyists. He looked up and down the lines for Mathilde. He knew she would be here, but where? It felt strange to be on his own at such a moment of collective significance.

The CGT representative's voice was calm, reassuring, at first. But then, as he spoke of poor wages, of the retirement age, of the injuries and accidents that had been occurring at the plant, his pitch grew more intense, his indignation plain.

There were thousands standing in that giant steel cave, listening. There was a sincerity in the air and, FB noted, very little heckling. He felt like an imposter, but by the time all the speakers had had their say there was a feeling of genuine optimism in the air. As the thousands poured out of the steel cave and back into the sunshine, a number of the chassis-monks downed tools to join them. By the entrance gates near the bridge a coffee van was doing a roaring trade. People stood about in large and small throngs, joking, humming bars of 'The Internationale', which had been sung with great intent back inside the shed.

FB made a note in his journal in 1988, some twenty years after that day on the island in the Seine, that it was apparently the first time in the history of the plant that 'The Internationale' had been sung there.

There was plenty of time before the march would begin from the Place de la République, but the momentum was already taking people back across the bridge towards Boulogne-Billancourt and beyond. After queuing at the coffee van for nearly half an hour, always with his eye out for Mathilde, FB stationed himself near the bridge to scan the departing crowd for her face. A dark-skinned man with a slogan printed on his t-shirt in Spanish thrust a wad of leaflets into his hand for distribution. Just as quickly the man was gone again through the crowd.

FB looked down at the roneoed information in his hand. It spoke of two hundred Algerians killed by the Paris police on the orders of its prefect in 1961. This had happened on, or about, the Pont Saint-Michel. The headline on the leaflet read: *'Où sont les morts, Papon?'*

FB knew that Maurice Papon was the prefect of police but he had not known about the two hundred who had died on his order in the very centre of the city. The look the man gave him as he handed FB the leaflets and the contents of the leaflets themselves had more effect on him than all the speeches he had listened to combined.

He began to hand the leaflets out as people crossed the bridge.

Later, he would wonder at his innocence as he stood

there amongst the sunlit thousands, handing out those pieces of paper seeking justice for the dead. He came to feel proud of that hour of his life but always felt ashamed of it as well. For in the precise moment in which he'd felt sure that for once in his life his actions were on the side of the vulnerable and the just, he was actually far more concerned with spotting a young woman in the crowd.

†

Maurice Papon was eventually tried in 1998 for crimes against humanity during the Nazi occupation of France. The Nazi hunter Serge Klarsfeld said during the trial, which was held down south in Bordeaux, the capital of *la France profonde*, that the French people would interpret a guilty verdict as indication that *'there is a limit, you must act on your conscience, even if you are a man motivated not by hatred but by procedures'*.

FB learnt later how in 1961 Algerian demonstrators had been bound hand and foot and thrown into the Seine to drown. He may well have asked himself whether that was regular police *procedure*, as administered by Papon, or police *hatred* resulting from the death of fellow officers at the hand of Algerians in the preceding weeks. Whatever the case, he knew nothing of all that as he stood by the bridge on the Île Seguin, scanning the crowd for Mathilde. But when the Algerian man had suddenly appeared from the crowd, coming right up to his face and handing him the pamphlets, FB could at least feel something of the horrors his people had endured, not only on the edge of the Saharan sands of their homelands but right there in the centre of a grasping, historic and intrinsically stylised Paris. And *why*, FB would ask himself later, *did that man choose me to distribute the leaflets?*

Perhaps it was FB's own vulnerability that saw him singled out for the cause: his, after all, was a vulnerability with no allegiance. Perhaps there was a blank, rather bewildered gaze on his face, a certain strangeness which in its unfamiliarity perhaps reminded the Algerian man of the purpose of his cause. They were both, in different ways, strangers, after all. And with those leaflets in his hand, bearing the question '*Où sont les morts, Papon?*', FB felt an unlikely complicity with a cause he'd had no prior reason to even begin to understand.

Or had he?

†

With respect to the proportions of the Haussmanian boulevards and their five-storey apartment buildings, and even despite the revolutionary barricades of history, the stimulus of 1789, 1848 and the Commune of 1870, the number of people assembled in Paris that day was unforeseen. FB handed out a few more leaflets and then moved across the bridge, making his way now back towards the metro and the Place de la République over the same ground on which cattle had once been driven before they were outlawed on the streets of Paris in 1828. Back then nature had been forced to make way, olfactorily, muddily, in all its desirous unpredictability, and this time, as the young FB Herschell emerged from the metro and approached the Place de la République by an unnecessarily circuitous route in the hope of sighting Mathilde and her friends, there was a different, less compliant writing on the wall. Such was the imposition of 'reality' on the moment that it felt almost as if the pre-1828 cows of a bucolic Paris might return.

He passed amongst an excited city suddenly prepared to express its distaste for the ultimate outcome of an original abstraction, for the cruel obfuscations and outmoded strictures of the Gaullist regime, by converting the arrondissements of the Left Bank into an artist book. The writings seemed now to be everywhere FB looked: scrawlings that had multiplied in humour and chagrin, in the living centre of the city. He read the walls and walked with what felt like the remarkable knowledge that he himself, with Mathilde, had made his own contribution to the living book.

La porte a été ouverte, mais l'oiseau va-t-il voler?

Nevertheless, as he approached the Boulevard Raspail he felt as if, unless he found her, he would remain on the outside of the tumultuous events, even as he stood amongst them. With Mathilde he could write on walls, contribute to the moment; without her, and now without the pamphlets he'd distributed, he felt like a hick, a loner, a *tourist*. And so the words Mathilde and he had written on the walls of the Rue de Buci began to twist in his mind until he felt himself like the canary in the *tabac* at Clamart.

FB walked slowly through Saint-Germain-des-Prés and crossed with the grain of the crowd towards the Pont Neuf and Rue de la Cité. In a few short hours the buses and cars would come to a standstill, the mass of people would be coming back along the streets in their millions, but as yet it was not entirely clear what would ensue. He took a detour to find the Rue de Buci and view their scrawled phrase, almost as a touchstone. Everyone was in groups, walking and talking volubly, but all there was to give him a sense of anything other than alienation were those words in the brown paint slightly discoloured by the blue.

He stood there for a moment, lit a cigarette and, a little pathetically, felt much better. One act of creation, the distribution of some leaflets, and the world became a place he could inhabit again. And yet, would he have ever written that phrase, and would he have stood for a whole hour distributing leaflets by the bridge, if he hadn't fallen in love?

Finally, as if drawn by the momentum of the streets beginning to surge with people all around him, he found his way out onto the Boulevard St-Michel and, savouring the memory of the pearl on his tongue, crossed the river.

8

Épanouie

THE MALAISE IN WHICH MATHILDE AWOKE ON THE
Monday morning of the Renault demonstration was
like nothing she'd ever experienced before. According to
the calendar, the weekend was over; normally she would
have had classes to attend, but the university was shut down
and the weekend, well, it seemed to have a lot more life in
it yet. If the fervour of the last few days was anything to go
by, France was about to experience the intense introspection of a holiday with no end in sight. And yet the whole
city was alive with an atmosphere not of introspection
but of catharsis. She felt as if, at last, some real work had
begun; the jemmying up of the cobblestones of the boulevards was not only a practical necessity of the moment but
also a perfect metaphor. Things had to be turned upside
down. Finally everything was being exposed to the spring
sky after years of an expertly administered darkness.

Mathilde herself had only been sixteen and still living at home on the Atlantic coast when the two hundred Algerians had been massacred on the Pont Saint-Michel. She had known about it through her parents. Her own mother had been born in Algiers into a French colonial, or Pied-Noir, family and, although a pacifist, had sent packages to the Algerian National Liberation Front, the FLN, as a younger woman. When in 1960 Albert Camus died in a car crash at Villeblevin, Mathilde's father had made a point of coming out fishing with his daughter on her *pinasse* to explain the contradictions of the man. With the narrow boat rocking under the celerity of the incoming tide, he told Mathilde how Camus had been against the Algerian war fundamentally because he was worried for the safety of his mother in Algiers. He felt keenly the humiliations that had been inflicted by colonialism and was philosophically aligned with the desire for independence, but refused to sanction a violence which included the torture of innocents and the murder of children. Thus, at heart, he was against both sides of the war. This man, Mathilde's father said over the hiss of the fast-moving skin of the *bassin*, was pure to an impractical degree. He was of course associated with the star intellectuals of Paris, Sartre and de Beauvoir among them, but was also a champion footballer with his feet very much on the ground. Such contradictions, Alain Soubret told his daughter, are the sign of a man you can trust. Camus had brought the reality of his love

for his mother like an untamed animal into the abstrac-
tions of the theoretical debate over colonialism. If you
ever, he called to her over the whistling and buffeting of
the rushing tide, meet a man who seems perfect, either
in body or mind, and who exhibits that perfection as his
primary gift, have nothing to do with him. In the flaw is
the human. Think of Camus, Mathilde. Use such a man
as your measure.

When the two hundred were massacred near the Pont
Saint-Michel the year after Camus died, Mathilde was not
that concerned about it. But her parents were. The blatant
savagery and significance of the act was not lost on them,
nor the fact that it failed to make headlines around the
world. They felt there was a secret France born not just of
racist colonialism but more fundamentally of *misanthropy*.
The police force in Paris signified the stubborn leftovers
of Pétain and his Vichy government. As a consequence
Mathilde's parents had refused even to visit Paris since
the massacre. When she left home to study there she went
with their blessing but, inevitably, with their worries and
chagrin as well.

The Pied-Noir community on the coast in Gascony was
relatively small, the Algerian community even smaller, but
in Paris, Mathilde wrote to tell them, there were people
from the edge of the Sahara everywhere. She began to
see her parents, though she did not write to tell them this,
as negative, hermetic. She encouraged them, particularly
her father, with whom she thought she might have more

luck, to come and visit her in Rue Monge. She was calling him out of the past and into the present. From *la France profonde* to *la France vraie*, from the traditional south where they were gasping for air to a city whose population truly reflected the superabundance of the country's history.

Her parents never came, of course, not even her father. He wrote to encourage her, both in her studies and in her hatred of de Gaulle. But he told her to be careful, too, and to avoid the police. They were not to be trusted.

Now she had seen this for herself during the night of the barricades. When the CRS riot squad had attacked at 2 am they had done so with violence and force, but more importantly with an attitude that implied things could get a whole lot worse. She had thought of the two hundred during those wild hours on the Rue Gay-Lussac. And she thought, too, of her parents' hermeticism down there by the rushing tides. What would it achieve, that burying of their heads in the sand? Or perhaps they had simply done enough and were now too old. Perhaps it was Mathilde's turn now, just as it had been theirs during the war. Perhaps.

She saw now that the malaise she was feeling had been seeded not so much by the night of the barricades but by her need to visit the Galerie Sarcon. Why, she wondered, as she lay in bed, unable to raise herself and make her way to the toilet, had she begun to make that same journey from her apartment in Rue Monge, along Saint-Germain and Saint-Michel to the gallery? When Georges, in his trenchant nostalgia for modernist art, had informed her that the early Mondrians would be on show at the Sarcon she had barely registered it. But the following day she found herself wanting to make her way there. And as the activity on the streets began to grow and she began to get more involved, her visits to the paintings became more and more frequent. This did not trouble her at the time, but now she began to see the connection between visiting the Mondrian dunes and her nostalgic talk at the restaurant of the *pinasse*.

She turned in her bed, away from the curtained window. She had agreed to meet Georges and Gilles at the cafe and from there go across to Boulogne-Billancourt and the Île Seguin but she couldn't move. Her body was like lead. She was horrified, conflicted, confused. If the layers of the city were finally being exposed in the streets outside, so too were the layers of her self right there in the darkened bedroom.

†

As far as I can ascertain from the contents of the boxes of FB's archive, it was not then the case with either of them that they, to put it in the jargon of pop culture, 'preferred his early work'. In different ways both FB and Mathilde's reason for returning to the Galerie Sarcon to view the Mondrian dunes was more personal and specific than aesthetic. It is clear that in FB's case he was studying dunes in order to stabilise antipodean roads, and these early Mondrian dunes, in their hovering at the midpoint between the figure and the abstraction of the figure, were, as Professor Lacombe had pointed out to him, almost unwittingly scientific. But it is also clear that Mathilde, having been born in the shadow of the Dune du Pyla, the largest sand dune in Europe, and having grown up on the shifting shores around La Teste-de-Buch and Arcachon, where the constant movement of sand reflected not only the nature of time but also the dynamic mutability of the culture and politics she was now experiencing, was homesick.

Mondrian had painted the dune pictures in Domburg, a Dutch town on the North Sea which, a little like Arcachon, had once been an aristocratic spa town where people came for a nature cure. From 1908 until 1916 Mondrian made annual visits, finding sympathetic conversation with the members of an artist colony of Dutch Luminists centred around the Indonesian born painter Jan Toorop. Toorop had himself been attracted to Domburg by the fame of its charismatic natural healer, a certain Dr Metzger, and also because the wealth of its summer nobility created potential buyers for his work. Together Toorop and Mondrian had discussed spiritualism and painting and, specifically, theosophy and Catholicism. In such nourishing circumstances Mondrian spent days on end painting amongst the dunes which, ultimately, he used as a key motif of his evolution towards the abstraction of nature.

The Mondrian dunes, as they were curated in the Galerie Sarcon, demonstrated clearly that it was amongst the dunes of Domburg, and in his conversations there with Toorop and other Luminists, that Mondrian began to integrate his theosophical beliefs with his painting techniques. He believed that naturalistic painting such as that with which he himself had begun was in fact a betrayal of deep reality in favour of superficial appearance. Thus he believed that naturalistic painters are often more interesting in their quickest sketches and studies than in their finalised paintings. This was because their intuitive or even unconscious aesthetic impulse contained more truth, and therefore more beauty, than their consciously finished, and therefore normalised, work. In a dialogue-essay Mondrian wrote many years after painting the dunes, and which I have been prompted to find a copy of since FB's death, he has a fictional naturalistic painter cry: '*Why did you discard all form?*' To which his fictional alter ego, a so-called 'abstract-real' painter, replies: '*When "things" are in evidence this always limits the esthetic emotion. Therefore the object had to be excluded.*'

Mondrian's Domburg dune paintings came early in his career. He is famous, of course, for paintings of vertical and horizontal intersections of primary colours, but before he had distilled his style down to the plastic originality that appealed to postwar America so much (remember the Partridge Family bus?) he dwelt for a time in a kind of conceptual littoral between idea and form. Therefore, or so it seems was the case as far as the owner-curators of the Galerie Sarcon were concerned, the dune paintings quite literally had it all. With their electric teals and tangerines, with their reduction of exterior expectations, they travelled out beyond naturalism; but with their retaining of the recognisable form of the dune in nature, they had not given up on the external appearance of the earth altogether.

†

She missed her rendezvous with Georges and Gilles, missed the demonstrations in the sky-high shed on the Île Seguin, as well as the slightly bewildered Australian handing out FLN leaflets near the Boulogne-Billancourt bridge. Instead she curled up in an armchair and read Nathalie Sarraute in a condition of torpor and shame.

By midday the gulf she felt between the hubbub she could sense on the streets outside and her own malaise was becoming dangerously deep. What was it, she began to wonder, about herself amid the shutdown of the city, that made her so sick and sad? After feeling so involved through the last few weeks, even as Georges annoyed her and Gilles was a pest, and even as her friend Josephine, who lived above her family's *boulangerie* on Rue Soufflot, had argued that it must all blow over and that they should get on with their studies so they would be well ahead when it all died down, she now felt as if she did not belong. The phrase that came to her mind was not one about whether the bird would fly now that the door of the cage had been swung open; it was more along the lines of *where* the bird would fly to now that freedom was in the air.

Escape. Even as the streets of the city were finally providing exactly that, she wanted more. She wanted a double escape.

†

I saw that the earth had become nothing. And there was one tear. Never had there been such a tear. (This tear, for me, was the sea).

Hélène Cixous

What was missing was the singable, edible, detestable land . . .

Hélène Cixous

9

Pioneer Vegetation

WHEN FB HAD FIRST ARRIVED IN PARIS HE STILL HAD the joke of his fellow violinist in the Moorabool Chamber Orchestra ringing in his head. Don Bryant was a Johann Strauss man, as unphilosophical as they come. He did, however, have a strain of dry humour that FB enjoyed and which saw them always gravitate towards each other during breaks in rehearsals. Once, when everyone, FB included, was very excited about reinterpreting Bruch's Violin Concerto No. 1, Don Bryant whispered out the corner of his mouth to FB that he thought the music sounded like the soundtrack to a mass grave. When FB informed his friend that Bruch was a renowned anti-Semite, Don Bryant's eyes had widened in mock indignation and he replied, 'Is that right? Well, surely there's no need to torture us gentiles as well.'

In February '68, the week before FB was to board his

Qantas flight at Essendon, he attended what would be his last rehearsal with the sextet. As word had got out about his trip to France, the well-wishers amongst his fellow musicians were effusive. Everyone was flattering and envious, except for Don Bryant. As FB was shyly explaining over sherry and sandwiches after the rehearsal how his trip was being partly funded by a French government scholarship, Don Bryant quipped: 'A foreign scholarship to go to sand school, eh? Sounds a bit like travelling to Scotland to study kangaroos. You do know there are a few grains of the stuff around here, Frank?'

The other Moorabool musicians managed a laugh at the joke, but they were also quick to make sure their mirth didn't go too far. The truth was that what Australians knew about France was confined to the vastly different feelings associated with, on the one hand, images of Paris as the beau monde, and on the other, the experience of war. Stories had been told, half told or gone untold in many families about the horrors of the winter quags of the western front in World War I and the generally perceived ambivalence of the French towards their occupiers in World War II. No-one much though had ever talked about sand. The idea of leaving the windy shores of Geelong, Bass Strait and the Southern Ocean to study sand in the shadows of Notre-Dame seemed rather unlikely. No-one however, except Don Bryant, had been impolite enough to point this out. And this was precisely why FB liked him.

When the young Australian had been walking to his first meeting with Professor Lacombe on only his second day in Paris, he held Don's joke in his mind a little like the grey gum leaf he had placed in his wallet as a reminder of home. And now, as he crossed the Seine on the day of the mass demonstrations, he could quite literally again smell the gumleaf dryness in Don's ignorant wit.

FB could hardly move for the human traffic. There were no buses, no taxis, it was all a moving shift of colours. This was not something that Don Bryant's dry humour could easily make fun of. It was not shopping, business, cowardice or tourism. This was a festivity of discontent. The general strike had only been called on the Saturday morning, with the injured of the night of the barricades still lying bandaged and sore in hospital, but somehow the short notice was necessarily in step with the urgency of the population itself. It was as if a hydrant had burst, spraying not water but people through the Haussmanian widths. An edifice of privileged comportment had been finally refused, and life had overflown its formats, spilling once again onto the streets.

FB did have an intuition of an endlessly repeatable historical moment but didn't of course properly understand the nuances of its eternal background. He stopped in a cafe in the Marais, stood at the bar and watched through the window as different tributaries of the crowd passed by on their way to the Place de la République, already with their banners and slogans up, with the spring in their step, the sun shining with pigeons flying over, and everyone sensing the time had arrived to put an end to the constriction of air.

In the cafe itself the owner and his regulars seemed excited too. There was no phlegmatism in this small business, only a sense of what FB's countrymen at home might have called 'a fair go'. The cafe owner, a thin man of about fifty, with a strawberry moustache but dyed black hair, was speaking rapidly of how there had been no Japanese tourists today and the police who usually took a croissant and coffee there every morning had not shown. Instead, he said, students ventured over the bridges – and strangers, he added, nodding subtly in the direction of the young civil engineer whom he obviously placed in a slightly different category to your typical student. This was not before time, he told his trusting interlocutors, who were all nodding in agreement. There are students blinded from the tear gas of two nights previous, he went on, students with broken limbs, and all because they had the good sense to overthrow the ridiculous old ideas and defend the Sorbonne against Papon's police.

After an hour of watching and listening, always with his eyes open for Mathilde, FB paid for his coffee and made his way back out into the street. It was strange to be at the heart of something of which he had only a distant understanding. From far away Paris had always seemed to him the home of the free mind and the free body. But this had quite clearly not been the case. The younger generations and the various ethnic minorities in the city felt betrayed, not only by the government but by its opponents as well. It was clear to the student leader, Daniel Cohn-Bendit (or 'Danny the Red', as he was known), and the students that communism, in all its sundry forms – Stalinism, Maoism, Trotskyism, even socialism – had sold out on the flexible dream of *liberté, égalité, fraternité*. The country was therefore in a moral and political narrow ditch. The surge of inevitable energy was finally bursting through.

As he came into the vicinity of the official starting point of the march at the Place de la République, the size of the crowd grew larger, its density thicker, and he had occasionally to work just to stay on his feet. From where he stood now he could hear chants and songs coming from the *place*: 'The Internationale', and various chanted slogans which amused him with their good humour. 'Guy Mollet, *au musée*' was just brilliant to FB – that a former socialist prime minister during the Algerian war could be consigned so emphatically to the dustbin not of history but of culture, in such a witty way. There was more predictable fare as well, such as '*Pompidou, démission*', or '*A bas l'état policier*', but in general the inventive humour of the slogans, particularly those of the various student groups, were revelatory to FB, in both their confidence and the way their originality cut like a knife.

He moved through the jostling streets until at around 5 pm, caught up in the progress of the main march as it moved towards the Pont Saint-Michel and the

Latin Quarter, he began to accept that the chances of sighting Mathilde amongst such an enormous number of people – was it half a million, or a million? – were slim. At this point his mood began to change, his fascination with the excitement all around him began to wane, replaced instead by a claustrophobia within the crush of the crowd.

But there was no getting out of the river just now. He was positioned right in the middle of the human stream as it crossed the bridge. But then, just as he was deep within the span over the Seine and about to step off with the crowd onto the Left Bank, the march stopped. Not knowing why, a slight rise of panic brought a sweat to his neck as his fear of the congestion of the crowd was compounded. Then the people all around him – to his immediate left a young man with wild brown hair and a t-shirt asking *Who Killed JFK?*; on his right a pair of middle-aged women who had been talking of hospital work as they had made their way along the route and whom, therefore, he assumed were disgruntled nurses; in front of him a gang of six or seven skylarking high school students; behind him a miscellany of smiling students – were all now bowing their heads, their expressions solemn. FB grew confused until, from up ahead, he heard through a megaphone that the pause was to pay respect to those who had been injured on the night of the barricades, those who lay in the hospitals even as the disruption continued, grew and blossomed. That was the word that was used in this solemn and unlikely pause; the dissent had blossomed, *épanouie*. The pain and suffering would not be in vain.

Standing there in the middle of Pont Saint-Michel, FB checked the remaining couple of leaflets he still had in his shirt pocket from the Île Seguin. It was true. Two hundred Algerians had died right here, only seven years previous. In comparison, the wounded of the night of the barricades were surely inconsequential. He frowned as he read again what the leaflet had to say. And in his mind he saw the face of the man who had sprung from the crowd to hand him the leaflets as he had stood scanning the island for Mathilde. What would that man make of this solemnity on the Pont Saint-Michel, of this marking of only the most recent conflict?

Suddenly he began to feel as if the whole day, the crowd, the historical momentum, was somehow childish. He looked to his left, past the boy with the wild brown hair. He looked right, across the profiles of the nurses' bowed heads and along the line of solemn sunlit noses. But no matter how far he craned his neck, or twisted this way and that, he could not see the water, the river. He was caught in the middle of something but he couldn't see beyond it. He was standing on the bridge right above it but he could not see it. There were just too many people.

†

From time to time, in later years, he would wonder how he had possibly walked away from it. It's clear from his papers that one of the strands of his interest became what he may have described as Cynical Literature, starting right back with Diogenes and coming into the present through Houellebecq. Thus he went via Huysmans and Benjamin, Fourier, Baudelaire and even Xavier Herbert, in order to explain that streak in him. In truth, it was this cynical streak that also took him towards 'the Thérèses', the two saints, one of Lisieux, the other of Avila. Anything that would help explain how he had stepped out of the river of people, away from the spectacle of the great situationist moment, was of great personal interest to him.

The feeling, the need that overtook him there on the Pont Saint-Michel, to squeeze his way laterally through all that human sunshine, to peel off through the various marshals of the various factional groups ushering the throng towards its destination at Place Denfert-Rochereau, was naturally bound up in attraction. As first his displeasure had risen at the ignoring of the two hundred dead Algerians, then because he couldn't see the water of the river, and then, finally, when this chagrin and desperation had congealed into a desire for what he could only describe as REALITY, it was then, and only then, that his sense of personal freedom found its emblem in the form of Mathilde.

Through the whole day, until that moment, his desire to see her had been automatic: he had been attracted to her, and it had something to do with the sense of connection she gave him to the city where he had come to study sand, the sand that was not there in Paris, except in archives and children's playgrounds. But now she was not there either, nor in the hours past, no matter how hard he looked. In her absence, she had loomed larger and larger in his mind so that, eventually, as he cast his eyes this way and that amongst the crowd crossing the bridge, he was not looking for her face any longer but for nature, for water, for the river that had brought not only the bridge but the whole city, and all those people, into being in the first place.

Amongst the millions on the streets he searched for an opening between faces, t-shirts, slogans; an opening that would lead him to the one amongst the many, a narrow side street away from the rebellious momentum, that would lead him not to aperçus and protestations but to where he could carefully state the interior thoughts he was having on the accumulations of the city, where he could pile words upon words until they became in themselves a rebel's barricade against distraction, a focus rather than an abstraction, a single kiss, a place in the city set free from those words by the silent moisture of a single pearl of saliva.

†

She likened it to the one day in history when she had stayed at home. When her mother was growing up in their well-off Pied-Noir suburb of Algiers, Mathilde's Grand-père Serreau had been obsessed with the high literature of France and particularly with Proust. The old man loved nothing better than to speculate, after lunch on a Sunday, and in rather dire repetition, on *À la recherche du temps perdu*, and how he himself might have behaved differently if he had been inserted into various parts of the action as a Pied-Noir protagonist. Mathilde had never been tempted to read Proust because her mother – her father too, in fact – had always presented him and his famous book as an insufferable bore. No doubt in Mathilde's mother's case this stance was somewhat influenced by Grand-père Serreau and his monologous Sunday delectations, but in Mathilde's father's case it had more to do with de Gaulle's rise to power after the war, and how the hypocritical maintenance of his power had forever infected the politics not only of remembrance, but of memory itself.

The anecdote that had stuck in Mathilde's mother's mind from Grand-père Serreau's Sunday repetitions – and which therefore had been passed down, albeit with a heavily grained family irony, to Mathilde – concerned that passage near the beginning of Proust's novel where Charles Swann, with uncharacteristic and immediately regretted frankness, proposes a scenario whereby the pages of the daily newspapers would be filled not with the titbits, sensationalisms and feuilletons you might expect, but with the text of a great work of literature, such as Blaise Pascal's *Pensées*. In this case, Swann declares, we would read literature every day of our lives, relegating the inanities of newspapers to the infrequency with which we might normally encounter great books – say, three or four times in our lifetime – and thus achieving a right balance between 'information' and 'publicity'.

A favourite game of Mathilde's grandfather was to imagine the very first morning when, as Swann would have it, the text of *Le Monde* had been replaced with Pascal's *Pensées*. In Grand-père Serreau's variation on the theme, he, as a Pascal devotee and a man of impeccable literary taste, refuses on that very day, and for the first time in his adult life, to buy the daily newspaper, in exasperated protest against the vacuities it contains. He walks straight past the newsstands and *tabacs* with his nose held high. And thus, at the Sunday table in Algiers, his putative scenario ends with his hands slapped to his forehead in mock dismay as he rues missing out on the very moment he had not, in his years of superior disillusion, even dared to imagine.

Mathilde's mother used to recall this anecdote once every couple of years while the girl was growing up on the saltmarshes of La Teste-de-Buch, only to highlight the multiple layers of personal hubris to which Grand-père Serreau was prone. She did, in fact, loathe almost everything about her father and his colonial ideals. But now his granddaughter, all those years later, on the geranium-coloured armchair under the window above Rue Monge, with her bedclothes pulled across the floor and wrapped around her midriff and legs, a small bottle of Coca-Cola on the table beside her, and Nathalie Sarraute's *Martereau* half read in her hand, revived the long-forgotten scenario in her mind. In actual fact, it came unbidden, almost like a family heirloom, in keeping with her own withdrawal from history.

The atmosphere out on the streets below was unavoidably charged, the festive, strident air could be felt almost physically through the window glass. There was also that strange absence of bus engines or other heavy traffic going by. There must be thousands, she thought, perhaps even millions marching out there, singing, calling out *De Gaulle, assassin!* and *Guy Mollet, au musée!* They would be laughing, chanting, all along the route from the Place de la République to the Place Denfert-Rochereau, spilling out into the squares, gardens and boulevards beyond.

And yet she, only she, stayed indoors. A young woman with her period, unable to bear the light; a young woman reading Sarraute in lieu of Pascal; a young woman mired and confused by her own memories; a young woman refusing the city's dream.

By the time FB had made his way with the crowd, moving again, down off the Pont Saint-Michel, she had stood up in her nightie and bedclothes and stretched her arms high above her head. As FB heard a small group crying *Sartre, au musée!*, he was slipping sideways out of the clutches of communal history, in favour of the side street of his own personal history. Meanwhile, she had swilled the last of the Coca-Cola and folded down the corner of the page of *Martereau* to mark her spot.

We lived in a studio on the Rue de la Grande-Chaumière, that was a change for me after having had every comfort; we froze in winter and in summer it was like a furnace. But how we worked! And the fun . . .

In the bathroom she changed her sanitary napkin and then washed her face in front of the bathroom mirror with a flannel.

On Rue de l'Échaudé FB breathed more freely as he headed south-east towards Saint-Germain and beyond that to Place Saint-Sulpice.

On the stairs going down to the street she felt her body's weight like a horse feels its rider. She wanted to shrug it off but she knew from experience that the revolution of her insides was an inevitable process quite separate from the mind or feelings.

As he approached Place Saint-Sulpice FB had the idea that, rather than return to his rooms, he should make his way to the Galerie Sarcon on the off chance it was open.

He looked at his watch as the canopy of the trees on the *place* shadowed him. He considered it unlikely the gallery would be open – it was 6.30 pm, after all – but decided to go anyway, on account of the fact that this was no ordinary working day keeping ordinary working hours.

She reached the street and stepped out into the soft evening light. Now she felt like a sleepwalker. Here and there people were coming away from the march, which was by now proceeding along the far diagonal of the Luxembourg Gardens. Here and there other people were walking towards it, perhaps trying to catch the speeches that would take place in Place Denfert-Rochereau. She turned left at Rue Notre-Dames-des-Champs, moving in the contrary direction. She could think of nothing else now but her *pinasse* and the winds blowing over the blond spits of the *bassin*. The ruffling of the water, the way the air created ribs of liquid, distressed her greatly. The beauty of her own past was returning to colonise her. She resisted, in her mind her heart her hips and womb, which groaned dully with every step. But she continued, moving further on her tangent away from the crowd. Sleepwalking. There was only one place she could go. To the place where the movement of the westerlies allowed the water to mirror the sand.

†

For a time they sat on different seats on either side of the Saint-Sulpice church without seeing each other. FB certainly *thought* of Mathilde. But Mathilde? Did she allow herself even to consider the one who had single-handedly set in train her strange crisis? Where did she imagine he would be at that hour, on that day, in that year, and in that city so far from his home? Was he in the midst of the chanting, was he caught up in the heat and joy of the situation? Had he climbed up onto a parapet near the

Luxembourg Gardens to observe what a revolutionary heritage really looked like?

No, he was quieter than that, less intrepid on city streets, and even likely to be frightened by the sheer volume of humanity. She understood. And yes, he had taken up a position in the south of her mind, like a single pine whose resin she simultaneously savoured and abhorred.

†

They saw it separately and only talked about it afterwards when they dared to anatomise their shame.

She rose from the warm stone of the bench beside the nave and set off amongst the flicker-flack of pigeons. She turned into Rue Palatine in order to hurry now to the gallery. She knew it was open until 8.30 pm normally but could not be sure, because of the strike, whether that would still be the case. She was winding her way through the streets, considering the dilemma of whether the gallery should remain opened or closed on a day of such collective freedom, when it caught her eye on the far wall of the street.

It shocked her. How could such a summation of her most personal feelings exist in such a public context?

SOUS LES PAVÉS, LA PLAGE

†

Under the cobblestones lies the beach. During the Second Empire, when Napoleon III was forever rearranging the city from a clutch of pokey narrow-laned heartzones to Haussmann's pristine wide boulevards, he knew the cobbles were a threat. To take the edge off, to defang the ready-made weaponry the people of Paris had used for centuries when rising up against such impositions, Haussmann arranged for wooden cobbles to replace the stone ones in certain sections of the city. But although the wooden cobbles made for less dangerous missiles in the hands of the displaced, it was still the case that the rain must fall, and the wheel, the horseshoe and the footstep must impress their weight upon the ground beneath them. Sure enough, the wooden cobbles would soon ruckle the roadways, buckling, splitting and bowing, frightening the horses, unsettling the carriages, even twisting the ankles of old watercarriers. Eventually, despite Haussmann's dream of disarming the ingrates, the wooden blocks had to be replaced again with the heft and durability of stone cobbles.

FB had had to pick the French words of the phrase apart in his mind until he could arrange them in a way that held both grammar and reason in hand. It was often this way. First he would see the phrase, then he would inspect and verify each word, and then allow them all to reconstitute back into the phrase.

SOUS LES PAVÉS, LA PLAGE

118

He smiled. He had walked past the heaps and mounds of cobbles with Mathilde, seen the ingredients of the barricades, and she had told him how they were hurled on the Friday night. He had seen the sand, too, with his own eyes and, strangely, thought nothing of it. But it was true. Under the reefs of cobbles lay the sand that stabilised the streets. The cobble bed. The paver's sand. The cobble's beach.

But now, in the brilliance of the late light of the day, he smiled for the way things had been reinterpreted. The poetry of the moment surprised him. How closely the scrawled phrase approximated his feelings.

There was something else, yes, and it lay within us, buried beneath the faces, the personalities, the cities we have made.

And he had this other thought as he walked beside the phrase written on the wall: even freedom can become a prison in the end.

10

Sand Gathers Around the Dead

EVEN AS I WRITE THIS I FEEL HIS STORY GRINDING DOWN like silica in my hands. His papers are blown sand, nibbled-at reefs, shingle on the shores of my imagination. Time, which often seems to be a synonym for wind, ruffles the sequence and softens the sharp edges. The moments that moved him, each moment as it relaxed or tightened his heart, is compressed down into the under-marl. What was active and dynamic in the margins of history's momentous day is manageable now, somehow smooth and rounded.

This is how nostalgia makes its inevitable case, this time for me to view FB and Mathilde as subjects of some hand-tipped picture postcard, or an oversaturated image offered up by Google, of two young lovers in the hip 1960s, touristic emblems presented by the Department for the History of Western Youth.

But sand isn't like that, it will not stay within the frame. And sand dunes – the forms that sand makes – come about not with open ease but in a turbulence created by limitation. They take shape, like young love itself, in the shadow of obstacles. It could be a wind-sculpted plant, it may be a dysfunctional family, or, in wider, more conceptual terms, it could find its form in the lee of a patriarchal resistance to a flexible proposal for the revolution of the world. Whatever the case, the sand as it formed in the shadow of the obstacle-personage that was known in 1968 by the name of *Charles de Gaulle* was made up of a million cellular impulses, organic motions, continuities and disjunctures. No longer would it suffice for the known world, or even a single coast of that world, to be painted as a mere copy of itself. The formerly invisible inner life had somehow now to be included: the life of the perceiver, the life of the wild, the neon of dreams, the catharsis of desire, the untheoretical edge of frustration. De Gaulle and his Compagnies Républicaines de Sécurité, or CRS, with their riot shields, their tear gas and batons, could not pretend any longer that the destiny of France was set in stone. The edifice itself was crumbling, the old regime granulating in a historical storm surge, its cobbles hurled back at itself from spirited, insouciant hands. Formerly unassailable heights were now scoured into valleys, alpine peaks crumbling off into the streams and sea-bound rivers of everyday life. And there, at the open mouths of the sea, the grains sifted along the coast, the same ocean coast of Western Europe where the young theosophist Piet Mondrian had painted the heaped-up grains onto canvases, characterising them as interiorised hummocks, lucid forms which decades later came to grace the walls of the Galerie Sarcon in the Rue des Quatre-Vents.

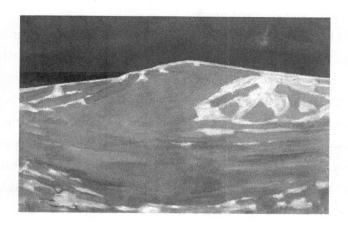

In Balzac's short story 'The Atheist's Mass', which he wrote in 1836, Rue des Quatre-Vents is described as *'one of the most disgusting streets in Paris'*. At that time Paris had yet to be reconstituted into Haussmann's boulevards and Rue des Quatre-Vents was one of those small streets that existed as squalid but beloved homes of the poor. By 1968, however, Rue des Quatre-Vents had well and truly entered a new epoch, along with the rest of the Rive Gauche, as a tourist destination tinted with cultural glamour. Even the fact that Balzac had mentioned it in 'The Atheist's Mass'

and in other stories from *La Comédie humaine*, such as *Lost Illusions*, gave it a certain lustre. This is the fetishisation of the historical ghetto, the Rue des Quatre-Vents as miasmic cradle and nursery to literary heroes. But when FB arrived at the gallery a few minutes after 7 pm he was thinking of none of that. Finding the gallery open he simply smiled to himself and stepped inside.

The small foyer was office-like, industrious, a little like the concierge counter of a small hotel. Typically Marguerite Tindel, the gallery owner, would be positioned behind the counter, tapping out publicity releases or other correspondence on her grey Olivetti typewriter, greeting customers as they came in to view the current exhibition, enquire about the next one or meet with her husband Jean on gallery business. It was sometimes the case though, that the only person she would see during the course of the day was a tourist asking directions to the Luxembourg Gardens, or the old postman Raymond, whose delivery of bills and overdue accounts at least came with a phlegmatic joke in his Bretagne burr, usually about the rudeness of bus drivers, who it seemed regularly attempted to mow the old postman's scooter down.

A few minutes after 7 pm, however, FB found not just Marguerite Tindel behind the counter but also her husband Jean, and three friends, all of whom were laughing gaily and drinking wine. They seemed almost surprised at first to see the young Australian in his overcoat enter but quickly assured him that although they had left the gallery doors open purely out of absent-mindedness, he was nonetheless welcome to renew his acquaintance with the Mondrians. But first, they said, he must have a drink with them.

Coming out from behind the counter, Jean Tindel thrust a glass of white wine into Francis's hand and, clapping him on the back, began to regale him with his own excited reflections on the day's events.

So when Mathilde peered through the glass doors of the Galerie Sarcon at approximately 7.15 she found that not only was the gallery open, but Francis was already inside, and not only was he already inside, but he was socialising, glass in hand, with the gallery owners!

Given that she had spent the whole day exiled in solitude in her apartment on the Rue Monge, trying to soothe the turgid motions of her ovaries and to ignore the mass demonstrations outside, she could only speculate as to what the momentous day had brought to the city, and how, or if, it would change the situation for students and workers, for the whole culture in fact. But she needed no further proof that the day on the streets had indeed been transformative than to see the shy, emotionally reticent Australian partying like a native with the bourgeois owners of the Galerie Sarcon.

This is, I suppose, the kind of misreading that can infect us when we take ourselves out of the loop. Suddenly it was as if there was not a public crisis occurring on the streets of Paris but a massive street party of which the little gathering in the office-foyer of the gallery was a satellite. And Mathilde had missed it all. What would she say to her father? 'Papa, I built my own barricade out of Coca-Cola and blankets, in solidarity with the revolution occurring within my body.' Or, 'The streets were filled with thugs and boors, the day would run its course. I decided early on that the only sincere and authentic course of action was to stay well out of it. Nothing I found in Sarraute contradicted that position.' She could hear her father's 'Pah!' already. She could also feel his confusion and disappointment.

For a moment, there on the other side of the glass, she thought about turning back. She would step away, immure herself in ordinary time, leave history to the bourgeoisie and the mob. She would step into her imaginary *pinasse*, sail back out of the Rue des Quatre-Vents, along the cross-currents and the turbulent shifting spits and shoals of the capital, until she would moor again at her own island on the Rue Monge.

It was so strange to even have such an impulse. She of all people. As the city of Paris transformed into a maze of sea lanes for her to sail in her childhood *pinasse*, something caught in her throat — was it a grain of sand, a clast? — and she pushed open the heavy glass door.

†

Once Mathilde had established that Francis had not suddenly become the most elegant and sophisticated young antipodean in Paris, a sense of normality returned to her. Turning with the others as she came through the doors it was immediately obvious that he was relieved to see her. As the introductions ensued it was clear that the Tindels and Francis Herschell were not so much bosom buddies of a revolution she had missed but mere acquaintances of a moment that would soon have passed. They had all been out there, from the Place de la République and across the Seine to Place Denfert-Rochereau. The gallery had been closed for the day and Francis had not of course been in to the university to prepare for his trip south. Nevertheless, they were not brethren of the Commune. In fact, they were all still looking for a connection.

One thing, however, did cement the common sense they had of the situation. With the arrival of Mathilde and the evidence that for herself and FB this amounted to some form of intuitive rendezvous, the gaze of Jean and Marguerite Tindel and their friends fell immediately, and fondly, on Mathilde and Francis as young lovers. The two of them felt the framework immediately. 'Oh, so you know each other! Oh, so you have both come again to where you first met, in front of Mondrian's dunes.' The pleasure the group took in assembling such a tableau was palpable.

So what did FB and Mathilde do in that situation? Did they, in the spirit of the day, react against this clichéd imposition and smash away and splinter the framework with their bare hands?

They did not.

After accepting a glass of wine from Marguerite Tindel and enduring a brief toast to the brilliant wit of Danny the Red, the 'young couple' were encouraged to proceed into the gallery proper to be alone with the dunes.

The lights in the gallery had not been turned on yet and for a few moments as they paused between the foyer and the exhibition space they stood in a half-light only hinting at the rectangular outlines of the framed pictures. But then they heard Jean Tindel cry, '*Pardon, pardon,*' as he hurried out from behind the counter to the set of four light switches by the gallery door. The switches were flicked. They heard the echo of the heavy clack of bakelite. There was a buzz, a splutter, and then all around them in the space the lights came on.

†

Sous les pavés, la plage. Under the cobblestones lies the beach.

They had seen the paintings before, but in an instant now they became the environmental source of their connection. Surrounded by Mondrian's dune slacks and slopes, and influenced by the nostalgic gaze of the Tindels and their friends, FB and Mathilde found a shared subset of the world.

But it wasn't as if they didn't also resist it. Slowly, first apart, then arm in arm, they moved through the space looking at the pictures. FB, still feeling very much like a hick at a private ball, momentarily heard the scratchy sounds of his own violin butchering the Bruch along with the other players of the Moorabool Chamber Orchestra. And Mathilde, caught by surprise, felt a stubborn discomfort inside her at being somehow patronised and cultivated, not by Francis but by the Tindels and their middle-aged sentimentality.

Nonetheless, what nature had heaped up at Domburg on the coast of Holland all those years ago did seem now like a halfway point, or compromise, between reality and the imagination. The dunes were cast anew not as sand but as plastic shapes of the painter's brush. Yet they remained too, and at all times, the accumulating dunes of Domburg. FB and Mathilde discussed the paintings as they moved around the room, smelling the sand of the dunes that the ideas of the paintings transmitted, feeling the sanctuary of this miracle-beach, where freedom from history, from all its heavily gridded lines, once again seemed possible.

Three

11

Polyp and Frond

S O THIS IS ALL I HAVE NOW: HIS PAPERS. EACH MORNING
I rise, have breakfast, and then drive along the road
Mr Lane built and that the young FB Herschell was
subsequently assigned to fix. I feel its solidity under the
tyres of my car and note the pleasing absence of a Bailey
bridge. I travel through the cutting at Point Roadknight,
over the bridge in Anglesea, up onto the ochre ridges
beside the defunct coal mine and through the back blocks
of the macrocarpa-sheltered farms heading north-east.
Eventually I make it into Geelong and park my car in
the usual spot next to the football stadium. From there
I cross the train tracks, walk up over the rise and down
to the small prime ministerial library at the university on
the edge of the water. I go to my usual table amongst
the shelves, beside which a trolley containing his archive
waits for me.

The boxes of the archive are loosely themed, but the papers are nevertheless wide and various. Slowly, day after day, the story has assembled itself in my mind, mainly through the miracle of his personal diaries of the time, but there are items, sentences, opinions and anecdotes in many of the other documents which pertain to what happened to him in France. And so I patch it together, reanimating the fertile mycelium I originally sensed under the pages of his book. I go travelling with him then to another country, another time, in which I take the liberty of seeking not only an explanation but a connection between what at first might appear to be disparate ingredients.

A man like FB, with a mind so alive, goes on a long journey, no matter whether he travels or stays at home. I'm trying to learn from that journey, to find the secret of his quiet harmonies even as I face up to the difficulties of the truth.

†

They snacked near Blois, some two hundred kilometres south-west of Paris, in a patch of forest on the Loire at Chouzy-sur-Cisse, where Professor Lacombe explained, as they sat in the car looking through trees onto the river, how in Paleolithic times the Loire travelled further north-wards and joined the Seine. Growing up in Rouen and mad for the natural world, Lacombe had studied what books he could find about the previous manifest of the landscape, all its slow changes. He had spent a period of time when he was about ten years old praying for a return to form on behalf of the rivers and alluvia, picturing in the unconstrained image-factory of his child's mind the ecstatic moment when the Loire would reappear out of the south, like some returning soldier from Aquitaine, to join again with his beloved Seine. Professor Lacombe wondered aloud then, as if inspired by the vast geological timeframe, about how the foment they had just left behind in Paris would be perceived in the long light of the earth's history. He proposed, in English, that it would amount to no more than a gust of wind. This was the very first indication on the journey of the long perspective which dominated the professor's mind. It certainly made an impression on FB, who mentioned it in his diary, with two exclamation marks after *'wind'*.

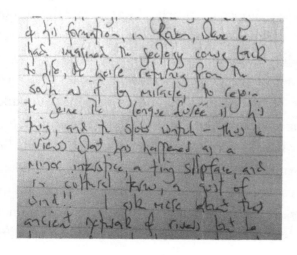

Mathilde sat in the front passenger seat beside Professor Lacombe. FB sat in the back, trying to follow the snippets of their French conversation and looking out the window as they pushed on towards the coast. Their destination was the Bassin d'Arcachon, at the northern end of the largest forest in Europe. This pine forest, which stretched southwards along the Atlantic coast towards Spain, was a key plank in what Professor Lacombe had been teaching FB, indeed in what FB had travelled all the way from Australia to see. It was an entirely man-made forest and could thank for its existence the persistent and massive tides of the Atlantic coast, which created the ever-easterly movement of the giant dunes around Arcachon, where Mathilde grew up. The grand revolutionary project of planting out two hundred kilometres of coastal wetlands with the aromatic and resinous *Pinus pinaster*, in order to turn the salted wastes, or *les landes*, into productive timber-bearing land was in part the idea of the eighteenth-century engineer Nicolas Brémontier. Rather ironically Lacombe called Brémontier *'Père des dunes'*, or Father of the Dunes, because it was he who received all the credit for the techniques that helped build up the dunes such as the Dune du Pyla, which now formed such a barrier between the ocean and the land. Before Brémontier's time, the miles and miles of sodden salt pastures supported the local community of marsh-farmers who made their way across their squelchy fields on stilts. But as the revolutionary era evolved, and an appetite for scientific progress increased through the 1700s, *les landes* began to be viewed as nothing-ground, as wasteland, which needed to be transformed into a productive agricultural purpose.

Lacombe's fascination with the area was clear. He had been visiting Arcachon for many years and in the front seat he now began to describe Brémontier's adaptation of local techniques whereby a mix of gorse and broom were planted with the resinous *Pinus pinaster* so that the slower-growing pines were protected in their early stages. Once the broom reached its limit at two metres, the pines, from their well-protected beginnings, began to shoot clear and to not only transform the marsh but bar the ocean by settling the sand into ever-rising foredunes. This work was aided by the erection of palisades, or slat fences, and also by the laying of brushwood over sand that had, crucially, been stabilised by the planting of *gourbet*, or marram grass. The mat-like root system of marram grass spread through the dunes like a powerful glue to hold them in place. Then, when under Napoleon III it was discovered that a bed of brown limestone fifty metres under the surface further restricted the drainage of the area, François Chambrelent, a successor of Brémontier, devised a drainage system of trenches, collection pools and the inclusion of cork and holm oak along with the pine. To demonstrate his techniques, Chambrelent had personally bought five hundred acres of sodden moor in *les landes* which he proceeded to transform. His achievement concluded what amounted to an epic engineering project which eventually saw the area become one of the richest in all of France.

Mathilde listened to the professor as they drove, occasionally correcting him on a village name or geographical misnomer. He was, after all, talking of the landscape where she had grown up and where her father's family had lived for centuries. Her family still lived, in fact, on the boundary of a remnant patch of salt pasture, or *prés salés*, at the oyster port of La Teste-de-Buch near Arcachon. It was from that squelchy ground that she had launched her *pinasse* as a girl. Lacombe was keen to question Mathilde about her family's history, most particularly when she mentioned that they still had her great-great-grandfather's marsh-walking stilts under the staircase of an old mill behind their house. FB noted how excited Lacombe was about that but he also noted how the professor's interest and enthusiasm seemed to alternately please and annoy Mathilde as they drove along.

By lunchtime they were in the small village of Saint-Florent-le-Vieil, where an old friend whom Lacombe had fought alongside during the war lived in a large house by the river. As Lacombe and his friend, a slim and cordial man named Louis Poirier, took their prearranged lunch in the house, FB and Mathilde bought fruit from the village and walked the sandy riverbank, discussing what Lacombe had been telling them.

An hour later they were on the road again, with Mathilde reading aloud from a newspaper Lacombe's friend had given them. She recited a list from the local paper which attempted to convey, rather than to summarise, the range of people who had been on the streets in Paris:

Railwaymen, postmen, printers, metro personnel, metal workers, airport workers, market men, electricians, lawyers, sewer men, bank employees, building workers, glass and chemical workers, waiters, municipal employees, painters and decorators, gas workers, shop girls, insurance clerks, road sweepers, film studio operators, busmen, teachers, workers from the new plastic industries . . .

As she read the list her voice modulated between excitement, pride and a melancholy brought about by her own non-participation. FB immediately brought up her involvement in the Night of the Barricades in an attempt to make her feel better. But Mathilde only smiled wanly, ignoring the too-obvious encouragement by retorting: 'It's a long list, but it doesn't mention civil engineers from Australia.'

†

Later that day, as the light began to slant west over the land of Poitiers-Charentes around Chevanceaux in the pre-dusk, they heard reports on the car radio of a strike at the Sud Aviation factory in Nantes. Mathilde leant in towards the dash, turning up the volume and glancing excitedly over at Lacombe behind the wheel. The news was significant, as it confirmed the possibility that what had happened in Paris could spread across the entire country. Nantes had always seemed to nourish the workers' voice; the workforce at Sud Aviation was heavily unionised, and it was no surprise therefore that it was in the vanguard of regional reactions. In the preceding months and years there had been lockouts of staff by management, redundancies, and much agitation within the intense factions of the unionised left. There had been a twenty-four-hour strike as recently as April, and in February, when earlier student demonstrations had been violently repressed by the police on behalf of the government, strong links had been established between workers and students. Repeated work stoppages had been planned by the workers at Sud Aviation, and the Force Ouvrière faction of the unions there had been pressing for another 'total strike'. Thus, when the repression and conflict exploded in Paris it was almost a fait accompli that Nantes would follow.

But what of the rest of the country, where, after all, conditions could not be so different? As they drove along discussing the likely scenarios, Mathilde assured Lacombe and FB that her father would know what was likely to happen, and where. Once they had passed south of Bordeaux and arrived at the coast at La Teste-de-Buch, he would no doubt update them thoroughly.

She was excited by the prospect of seeing her father, FB could see that, excited also by the sense of vindication she felt sure her father would be receiving from the events. And this was where FB felt both helplessly in love and hopelessly out of his depth. Although she was younger than he, Mathilde was no fool, and there was no escaping the fact that FB was far from politicised. But he was increasingly attracted to the worldview Mathilde had been brought up on, whereby the ordinary human of everyday life was continually cannibalised by those who had no more meaning in their life than an obsession with power. The truth was a bifurcated thing: on one hand it was in the urgent eyes of the Algerian who had thrust the leaflets into his hands near the bridge at Boulogne-Billancourt; on the other hand it lay in a far more inscrutable reality to be found in the slowness and stillness of dunes, whether they be real or painted.

He already understood that this bifurcation was the very territory where the connection between himself and Mathilde lay. In Paris she had helped assemble the barricades, shielding her eyes from the tear gas and hurling whatever she could find at the perspex shields of the CRS. She had done this all night long and was as strident in the dawn as she had been before the unknown horizons of midnight. But then she had faltered. Or deepened, depending on how you looked at it. She was fighting against the depth and he was part of that struggle. She had made her way to the gallery, she had held him and let herself be held. She had agreed to forgo the dramatic public moment in favour of the relative quiet of the south in order to travel with him and the professor back to the homeland of her upbringing. But even so it was all still up in the air, all in jeopardy still, nothing was resolved. FB's skin was tingling permanently as a result. Everything felt both electric and ambiguous. He was approaching a coast unknown to him, where his professor and Mathilde would, in different ways, be the experts. He would be the apprentice, both in his studies and in love, and as he looked out the rear window of Lacombe's car and caught sight of the *Pinus pinaster* for the first time, it occurred to him that he had waited his whole lifetime for what he was about to learn.

†

Mathilde had been irritable as they'd bypassed Bordeaux but she grew calm and silent as they cruised down the motorway onto *les landes* and approached La Teste-de-Buch. She began to point out things in the landscape, turning towards the back seat to show them – to show them off – to FB rather than to Professor Lacombe. Now that they had entered a space wherein the sky seemed higher, vaster, she may have assumed that the Australian would relate. He, not the Professor of Sand from the University of Paris, would have the eyes to see. Perhaps she looked at the landscape now with something of those imagined eyes herself, as well as her local knowledge, and as FB responded enthusiastically in the back seat (he did note in his journal that finally, after many weeks in the congestion of Paris, he felt he could *see* and *breathe*) the rapport between them would surely have been palpable to Lacombe. This was a young woman showing her beloved the things she loved the most: the remnant russet swamps between the planted pines, the roadside oyster stalls – and they still hadn't even made it to the coast proper. FB also noted that, for the first time on the journey, '*Lacombe must have had the annoying sense of being a chaperon*'. FB wondered, too, as they drove through the small town of Marcheprime, whether the professor might even forbid Mathilde from accompanying Francis on their field research upon the dune.

†

The hotel the professor liked to stay at in Arcachon was the Loup Garou, in the Ville d'Hiver, or winter village. This was on the hill above Arcachon, some distance from the salt pastures and oyster beds of La Teste-du-Buch, and so Lacombe took a detour to drop Mathilde and Francis at Mathilde's family home before continuing on his own in the car to the Hotel Loup Garou.

Thus, on the casual footpath of the coastal town, the two students stood briefly with their bags, alone and nervous, both feeling like adolescents again.

They were surrounded by a burgeoning suburb ringed by empty salt fields. Close by and in the distance boats were marooned in the mud by the notoriously low tide of the fishing port. Immediately before them stood a low, modest Basque-inflected house amongst pine trees, a house with whitewashed walls and with a low whitewashed concrete fence separating it from the road. Behind the house was a sky so softly blue it surprised FB to find it by the ocean.

Mathilde told FB how strange she felt to be home. She knew her father would be excited to engage with a visitor from Australia but knew also that he would be disappointed that she had left behind the momentousness of Paris. On the other hand, her mother would be glad that she was out of harm's way, knowing as she did that no revolution ever succeeded without bloodshed, injustice and brutality. Mathilde warned FB that when it came to the issue of him her mother would be nonplussed, interiorised, shy.

They had raised her safe in La Teste-de-Buch, amongst the sea lanes and oyster beds. La Teste and the entire locale of the *bassin* had a strong patois, a deep identity, but it depended in its laconic, phlegmatic attitudes on the fact that whatever cultural mask it wore was constantly being adjusted by the direct immensities of nature. Thus, it would accommodate certain inflections, immersions, tones, only to have them suddenly divested, exposed or stripped back, always and every day. For those who had been around Arcachon for more than a few generations, any external scheme to develop the port, any grand external show of certainty or egoist aspiration was met with resignation, humour or outright derision. All of which made sense to Mathilde's mother, whose volatile childhood in Algiers had stayed with her like a rocky ballast, stabilising her in the truth of conflict, its dangers and perpetuities, and therefore allowing her to maintain solid coordinates even amongst the loomings and change-ability of the Gascony tides.

For his part, FB was positively fizzing there in front of the Soubret house. Lacombe had begrudgingly agreed that FB could save on accommodation costs by staying in the old *moulin*, or mill, behind Mathilde's parents' house, but FB felt a degree of truancy in relation to his sepa-ration from the professor nevertheless. When Mathilde smiled, took his hand and leant in to kiss his cheek before they entered the house, he was also concerned that her parents would see them. If they were outside *his* family house on Milipi Avenue, such affection would have been unthinkable. The sharp austerity of his home, where open affection was always uncomfortable, would have made sure of that. But here he was reminded that such displays were not embarrassing or criminal. They were, in fact, the point of it all. Even the weather, in this case so easily blue and white and clear, seemed to FB at that moment to be a space coaxed into existence by romance.

†

Beyond the southern whitewash of the facade and front fence FB found the interior of the house warm with polished wood and comfortable furniture. And books. More books than he had ever seen inside a family home. They lined the airy tiled hallway leading from the entrance into the core of the dwelling; every glimpse he had into the rooms they passed along the way seemed also to be filled with books; and in the living area itself, with its low ceiling of exposed pine, the largely white paper spines were again the feature.

This was not what he had expected, nor was the imposing figure of Alain Soubret as he met them at the door. Mathilde's father was an unusually tall man, easily taller than the six-foot Australian, with a strikingly gaunt face. His black hair was swept back from his high forehead and to the side, his eyes were a sharp blue and his body still firm, young-seeming, though thin. Surprised as Alain Soubret was to find his daughter on the doorstep, he quickly subsumed his disorientation, his disappointment even, into the warmth and affection of fatherly love. And with that fatherly love came a warm welcome of his daughter's guest.

After coffee in the kitchen at a dark round table shaded by a large fig tree outside the window, and a conversation which touched briefly on the state of play in Paris, and also in Nantes and Lyon, but much more on the purpose of Francis's visit, Mathilde suggested to her father that she show FB out to the *moulin* in the garden.

Alain Soubret agreed, telling FB that the mill would not only be comfortable but a quiet place in which to write up his notes after his field trips to the dune. 'Make yourself comfortable,' he said, 'and then later you can come back in and dine with us. Mathilde's mother will be back by then, and we can get to know you a little.'

At which point Mathilde hugged her father, kissed him on the cheek and, smiling, made for the double doors to the garden to lead FB to the mill.

If a life's significant moments are ground down from the ephemerality of time acting upon the materiality of space – wind on rock, liquid tide on cliff and shore – until a grain of memory is formed, then one such grain was about to take shape in FB's life. It would not exist in isolation, of course – already the day had become indelibly *heaped* with significance – but just as one jagged edge of quartz can catch the light where the equally gregarious grains around it cannot, so it was that a momentous day was about to receive the glinting centrepiece around which the infinite grain-moments of its duration would gather and form.

By now it was four o'clock in the afternoon. She took his hand (his brown suitcase was in his other) and led him through tumbling green, a garden rumpled and hirsute, with as many fronds and leaves and tendrils as there were books inside the house. Many more, in fact. The sun had reddened some forms and merely brought more of the green out in others. Through it all ran a hand-mown path, at the end of which FB could glimpse a circular building whose buckled circular stone walls seemed in keeping with the tumblings of the garden itself. After the long motorway south, everything seemed suddenly rounded and strewn, quite the opposite to the effect achieved in the Jardin des Plantes in Paris, where FB had wandered like a solitary in the first hours and days after his arrival. The Soubret garden felt to him like something unintentional, evolutionary. His brief journey through the book-filled house, from front door to back via the hallway and conversations in the dark cave-like kitchen, had been tense and polite, but now the Atlantic sky reclined behind the irregular column of the vertical stone-and-daub *moulin* as if content with his progress. Mathilde's father did not follow, and her mother was out collecting shellfish at the shore. They were alone.

✝

For the young Francis Herschell the mill became immediately a double interior. On approach it seemed a relic whose engineering vernacular momentarily fascinated him. Most likely built from local stone, it was roughly daubed, irregular, but certainly round. The tints of the stones were dark and variegated against the lighter slurry of the daub, giving the effect of coarse gems set in ascending patterns of white earth. But once he and Mathilde had entered under the dark and slightly askew lintel, through a narrow timbered entrance into a rustic kitchen with a wood stove and white, roughly plastered stone-cut walls, he felt the excitement of having entered into the living space of another distinct culture. Hence the doubling effect: alone with Mathilde he had also entered into the historical privacy of *la France profonde*.

On the left there was a spiral staircase leading up out of the kitchen to a sitting room above, and then winding even higher again to a bedroom on a third level. Francis's eyes immediately fell on the possibility of the bottom step. Well, he would have to be sleeping up there, he presumed, for the tiny kitchen and a bathroom at the back took up the whole ground floor of the structure. He became aware of the erection growing in his pants. In fact, it was not so much growing as instant. He could smell Mathilde standing beside him and sensed the weight and flex of her body. 'My *grand-père* restored this building,' she told FB. 'It was long ago a working mill for grain, but in the end he lived in here as an old man when my father returned home with my mother. I remember him at the stove here when I was a young girl. And at this table. He liked to play chess and to garden and cook. He made wine also. He died in his sleep in the bed upstairs.'

'Was he political?' FB asked.

'Like my father? No. But he had a local mind and grew annoyed by the pace of change. At times this annoyance was in sympathy with my father's interests, at other times they were opposed. But no, his interests lay elsewhere, though naturally he was active in the resistance after Hitler invaded.'

They were standing by the round table in front of the

stove. She smiled. 'I think that he would not disagree with what has happened these last few days,' she said. 'Though I'd have to ask my papa. Perhaps at the very least he would have liked *sous les pavés, la plage*. He would have joked about how long it has taken everyone to realise that. He might also have added, *sous l'eau se trouvent les huîtres*. Under the water lies the oysters.'

†

FB's brown suitcase stayed downstairs, alone on the equally brown patina of the painted stone floor of the mill's kitchen. The two of them ascended.

They climbed past the sitting room and lay amongst the shadows on her *grand-père*'s high bed, wooden shutters flung open but barely letting in any light. She had continued with her memories of the old man, giving herself over entirely now to a nostalgia which afterwards she would come to view as symbiotic with their sex. Francis listened, pent-up but in heaven, trying to disguise the ruckle in his Fletcher Jones trousers.

Before long Mathilde's descent from cultural urgency into regional nostalgia was transposed into their mutual desire for each other. For a time, though, they continued to fuel this desire by masking it with the charms of a rustic past, which they could still smell in the mill: the leather of a bellows, the deep irregular sills, the musty rugs, the silt and sedge of the salt pastures that stretched from where they lay, beyond the leadlight of the windows, to the shores of the *bassin*. They were freed by the atmosphere to recount stories of home and childhood, FB even venturing briefly into a fishing anecdote from a long-ago spring. So May was November, she remembered. Yes, his world was upside down, and that's when she silenced him with her lips.

Now Mathilde's skirt rode up above her knees, one of which she threw across FB's midriff as their conversation ended. He did not know how experienced Mathilde was, but he knew that he most certainly was not. She sensed as much and he felt it excited her more. In truth, she had had sex with her cousin Michel at Cap Ferret on the far side of the *bassin* a number of times before she left for Paris. She had kissed Georges, too, in her apartment on Rue Monge when she first met him, before she knew what a pretentious boy he was, but that was all. Her red hair fell across FB's face with the wild undulance of the garden.

He felt like he might implode but she coaxed his tongue into her mouth as a temporary release. Their mouths twirled and adventured. He began to seek her out too, her under-curve and then her hard nipples. As her fingers roamed inside his shirt, he grew consciously embarrassed by how his singlet spoke of his life in Geelong. It was hot, after all, even if it wasn't as stifling as Paris; it was too hot for a singlet. He quickly shed his own habit. There was a rumour that somewhere deep in the past his own

Herschell ancestors had originally emigrated from western France to Ireland, but it was pale Irish-Corio skin that now became exposed in the brain of the mill. His cock chafed as she kissed his chest as lightly as the fluttery wings of a willie wagtail.

When he entered her underpants with his hand she grew serious. Even sombre. The mood deepened and he slid his forefinger easily between the slick of her lips but dared not go inside her. She kissed him harder now, as if the tragic star that momentarily hovered above Paris could only be understood through this immersion in the transience of sensations. With one hand she began unbuttoning her own blouse. He began to help her. Her eyes caught his. His fumbling fingers confirmed his innocence. This was no game, no sparring or jousting. He had travelled for sand but this was what he had really travelled for, and he knew, in a moment so fleeting that he barely noticed it, that this single glowing grain of time had just changed him.

One moment we are ascending, a million separate cells abuzz and seeking. The next we become unified, the particular singularities that we are.

Sensing his disillusion she burrowed into him. Soon her hand was there on his zip and springing him free. Dim shadows oxidised, vapours trailed, sharding darkness to emotional light. She longed to mount and have him go into her.

He tugged at her underpants and released her. Down

she went until she rose up again, this time pendulous, freckled and grinning. Looking straight into his eyes she wore him like a polyp, a sleeving thing, so easy. Her skin went pale as she shimmered like silk. When finally he sought her hilt she fell towards him in gusts. Tightly they clenched, closing into one form like the two living halves of a shell. Then they laughed and exhaled.

12

Dérive

GASCONY RAINWATER HISSED ON THE WOOD STOVE downstairs. Outside the mill stood an Occitan tank, all stippled and worn but well made, into which Mathilde's *grand-père* used to pump water from a well in the garden. But from the yard now the water ran pressured through the taps over the sink, like news channelling through a radio. She filled the teapot and placed it on the stove she'd lit when she first came down, humming 'Being for the Benefit of Mr Kite' as she did so.

FB lay upstairs, in a mood halfway between bliss and stupefaction. He could not have cared less if she became pregnant; they could shack up in *le moulin grand-père* and run charter boats out into the Atlantic. He would gain a second education amongst her father's books and all would be well.

And to think they'd only just arrived.

He was due at Lacombe's hotel at 7 pm for dinner and a quick preliminary discussion on what they would encounter the following day, though nothing with Lacombe ever happened that quickly. Still, he could drink a coffee with Mathilde, borrow her bicycle, and cycle the three kilometres around the port of La Teste-de-Buch into Arcachon to meet his professor. Mathilde had assured him that her parents wouldn't think him rude. He was working, studying, he'd come from the other side of the world. From miles beneath their feet, in fact. There would be time to meet them properly in the next couple of days.

When he came downstairs she was smoking a cigarette in the open doorway, under the skewed lintel. It was the only source of light on the ground floor. FB reached for his suitcase so he could change, and as he leant over she reached across and placed the cigarette in his mouth. He inhaled, she withdrew it from his lips. She told him that she liked his lips very much and stared at them now, with extra intensity. They drank coffee while twining their fingers across the dark wood of the round table.

†

Before FB left the house he had the opportunity to meet Mathilde's mother, who entered the garden through a back gate just as he and Mathilde were emerging. Madame Soubret, a short, strong-looking woman, stood frowning at them with a wooden bucket full of oysters in one hand and the bright sleeve of an LP in the other. She wore a denim shirt and unusual pantaloon-style trousers which buttoned just below the knee, leaving exposed thick and tanned calves.

Mathilde was certainly not effusive at the sight of her mother but nevertheless they embraced and Francis Herschell, the young Australian civil engineer, was introduced. *'Il est là pour étudier les dunes,'* Mathilde told her mother, who managed to smile politely while raising an eyebrow.

'Un grand sujet,' she observed.

Mathilde turned to FB with amusement on her face. 'She says the dunes are a rather endless field of interest.'

FB was already smiling, having understood the sardonic nature of what was said. Now though, he lowered his eyebrows and creased his brow. Turning to Madame Soubret (there was no 'please call me Madeleine') he nodded and said, *'Oui, oui, ils sont.'*

†

A few minutes later, when he was cycling alone towards Arcachon and the Hotel Loup Garou, FB noted the way the resinous pines that lined his route gave way on the high ground of the Ville d'Hiver above Arcachon to stately elms and oaks. He dismounted halfway up the ascent and caught his breath. He looked back down the Avenue Leon Gambetta over the beachfront streets of Arcachon, across the stately nineteenth-century promenade and jetty beyond the post office and across the water rushing back into the *bassin* between Arcachon and the low-lying peninsula of Cap Ferret. These were Mathilde's home waters, and he saw too how the *bassin* bore no small resemblance to his own Corio Bay back home. On the lookout for convergences, he made quick topographical calculations comparing the Bellarine Peninsula with Cap Ferret. He concluded that although Port Phillip and Corio represented a larger scale indent into the ocean coast of Bass Strait, they were nevertheless of the same geomorphological stamp. This surprised him, and had the added bonus of making him feel somehow more at home amidst the revolutions of his heart. He resolved to discuss this issue with the professor with respect to the application in Victoria of the dune stabilisation methods used in Arcachon and Cap Ferret. To the eye of the novice, at least – for that's what FB was at this stage – the similarities between the Southern and Atlantic oceans pounding the shores of the coasts protecting the bays of Port Phillip and Arcachon had to suggest the potential of shared physical applications. It was clear that the velocity of the tides was a factor of considerable differentiation, but even so he found a certain mirroring effect involving treacherous waters issuing through a narrow indentation in the land uncanny.

Turning away from the view, adjusting the satchel on

his shoulder, he continued pushing the bicycle up the hill. Three-quarters of the way up he veered right into Avenue Victor Hugo, and after another few hundred metres or so of the shaded tranquillity of oaks and elms he found the Loup Garou set back in a garden on the high side of the road.

The hotel was tall and striped in coloured stone. He climbed the steps and, entering the foyer, found the professor waiting for him, dressed in a light brown summer suit and looking relaxed despite the long drive. He greeted his student warmly and suggested they take an aperitif in the front lounge.

To FB's great surprise the front lounge of the Loup Garou was a room almost entirely given over to the cartography of the Bassin d'Arcachon. Amongst comfortable couches and chaise longues dotted around a mosaic floor, the professor chose a small table from where they looked through large windows across the botanical slopes of the Ville d'Hiver and over Arcachon and the bay to Cap Ferret. Immediately the view captivated FB and his satisfaction was quickly trebled as he noticed the array of framed local maps adorning the walls. His eyes were widening as he took them in and, looking on, the professor smiled at his obvious pleasure.

'*Alors*, through the windows we have the subject in nature and on the walls its strata of cultural interpretation.'

FB nodded slowly, also with a smile. 'I see,' he said, dumbfounded.

A waiter appeared at their table, and after a brief consultation the professor ordered a glass of orange wine for them both.

Even at such a distance (the hotel must have been some three kilometres as the crow flies from the shore), FB could see through the windows the hydraulic heft of the tide pouring into the *bassin* from the Atlantic. Lacombe began to relate the tragedy of *lou gran malhour* of 1836, when almost the entire fishing fleet of Arcachon and La Teste-de-Buch had lost their lives trying to re-enter the passes of the *bassin* in a wild Palm Sunday storm. As FB looked out at the water, small boats were beating both ways in the current, seemingly at the mercy of the tide. It was easy to visualise how precarious the passes into the bay might become in even stronger weather.

As it was the early evening was mild. When the wine arrived Professor Lacombe got up from his chair and motioned for FB to do the same. Walking over to the eastern wall he began to point out the rationale of each different map of the *bassin*. Some of these were copies of maps of great antiquity; there was even a diagram of the bay's contours dating from 1302.

The maps included outlines of the Arcachon town plan, overviews of the shores of the *bassin*, and were, as the professor pointed out, invaluable for the changes they showed. Some also included the Dune du Pyla, which stood approximately three kilometres south of the hotel. It was notable for how little it had changed compared to the rest of the *bassin*. On most of the maps Pyla remained a solid, rectangular wedge at the southern mouth of the bay, and even as the sands of the treacherous passes leading into the *bassin* shifted about in time, the *Grande Dune* stood almost like a disconnected entity, piled up grain by grain like a bookend of the bay.

The professor then led FB to the western wall of the lounge where, along with more maps of the *bassin*, were hung many historical photographs and postcards of Arcachon, La Teste, the Dune du Pyla and Cap Ferret. FB's eye was immediately drawn to a sepia postcard of two '*parqueuses*', or oyster women, standing amongst the racks at low tide wearing the same style of pantaloons that Mathilde's mother had been wearing back at the mill. When he mentioned this, the professor raised his eyebrows and remarked that the *parqueuses* were well and truly a thing of the past.

What the professor wanted to show FB on the western wall, however, was not the postcards and early photographs but a series of charts mapping the sand forms of the passes over the course of the centuries.

'When I first stayed here,' Lacombe told FB, 'it was 1952. The Ville d'Hiver was still somewhat stigmatised by the tubercular reputation it had acquired during the years when Arcachon was viewed as a climatotherapeutic destination. This room of maps fascinated me and of course is the reason I continue to insist on staying here, despite the expense, whenever I am in the area. After I had been here a number of times and got to know Monsieur Draguignan, who had single-handedly researched and curated the objects in this room, I was audacious enough to suggest to him that the sand diagrams of the area which I had discovered in the archive in Paris would make an appropriate addition. Monsieur Draguignan agreed to view them and so, when I returned to Paris, I spent a series of enjoyable evenings composing decorative copies of them in my flat. When Draguignan saw them he was delighted, and so, happily, here they are.'

These charts of the passes were mounted in a grid of nine squares, three across and three down, each of which contained a depiction of the indentation into the Atlantic coast. The first image, in the top left-hand corner, was from the 1300s. It depicted the ancient river Leyre, which caused the coastal indentation in the first place. The last image, in the bottom right-hand corner, showed the *bassin* as it existed in 1965, just three years before Lacombe and FB Herschell stood inspecting the charts in the map room of the Hotel Loup Garou.

Lacombe had hand-inked the hydrological maps in a scientifically accurate but nevertheless pleasantly orna-mental fashion, in order that they would be in keeping with Draguignan's rather sumptuous room. Thus, the sandbanks in each of the images were represented in a pale apple-green, the dunes in an apricot-tinted yellow, and the water in off-white. The currents and directions of the channel flows were inked in what FB would have called royal blue but which could fairly be described as a traditional Arcachonaise blue. Each shape or outline, including the dune heads and the banks of sand within the mouth of the inlet, were bordered with a delicate thin line of bright orange Indian ink.

The earliest image, of the Leyre in full flow, like all the subsequent images, was a morphological estimate based on the navigational and hydrological maps kept by the Société Historique et Archeologique d'Arcachon. These estimates were made by the Bordelaise hydrographer Jean-Pasquale Mosquito. Mosquito's earliest image showed the Leyre with its wide mouth opening directly westwards into the ocean, its flow only obstructed by small islands of sand spaced at flotilla-like intervals between its banks.

The second image, which estimated the contours of the *bassin* some three hundred years after the first image, showed how the southern dune head had encroached to the north, obscuring the wide opening so that, with the fingerish tip of Cap Ferret reaching down from the north, it begins to resemble the treacherous mouth of the bay as it was in 1968.

The third image, the last in the top row and dated around 1400, showed the southern dune head changing shape so that it extended further to the east in a bulb-like peninsula, further narrowing the channel between the northern and southern dunes.

In the first image of the second row, dated at 1708, were visible the consolidations of the original smaller island in the Leyre into what was now called the Île aux Oiseaux, or Island of Birds. This was set back deep into the *bassin* from the heads and began to create the two-channel formation of the modern era. Importantly, this chart of 1708 was also the first in the sequence to depict the massive Dune du Pyla in the southern head, which formed as a direct consequence of the onshore westerlies blowing sand from a low tide bank, now known as the Banc d'Arguin, across to the eastern shore. In this 1708 image the Banc d'Arguin had still not fully severed from the coast proper but nevertheless had begun to form a fish-hook shape running north-east to south-west, which ultimately saw the belly of the hook eroded and the bank left as a separate entity in the passes.

In the following image, from 1829, the Banc d'Arguin had broken off from the shore and, with the curl of Cap Ferret further eastwards across the entrance, began to show the passes that had claimed so many lives just seven years later in the *lou gran malhour.*

By 1912, FB saw, a pattern was beginning to emerge between the northern and southern channels, which narrowed and widened in alternate fashion. By this time, of course, Arcachon was well into its aristocratic heyday and the interests of developers and industrialists had begun to conflict with those of the local fishing community. Time and again during the period between the charts of 1829 and 1912, the fishing community insisted to the entrepreneurs that the ephemerality of the passes was such that Arcachon could never, as they dreamt, be transformed into France's largest industrial port. Time and again the developers refused to listen. Inevitably, the fishermen and women were proven correct and chart by chart on the wall of the map room in the Loup Garou displayed concrete evidence of the treacherous facts. By 1965, the date of the final image, in the bottom right-hand corner of the grid, the Banc d'Arguin had reduced somewhat in size and the northern channel by Cap Ferret had become almost impassable. On the southern shore, however, the Dune du Pyla just continued to grow, courtesy of Brémontier's plantings and the velocity of the tides exposing the sand of the Banc d'Arguin every six hours to the scouring Atlantic westerlies.

The professor proudly pointed out how the sand charts he had copied so expertly during those long evenings in Paris were a representation of the key determining factors of the evolution of the town of Arcachon, with its many and complex layers of fishing, climate therapy, casino tourism and so on. 'Arcachon has a distinct and deservedly famous human culture,' Lacombe declared to FB with a steady look, 'but at heart it is all about the passes and the sand.'

They returned then to sit at their table and sip their wine. FB could see how perfectly happy Lacombe was in the conducive environment of the Loup Garou, and now, with a sweep of his arm that took in the view through the large window, the professor simply said: '*Voila.*'

It was true enough. There in front of them were the passes themselves, with the tide visibly rushing in, and pleasure boats and fishing boats and even the bright red ferry to Cap Ferret negotiating its vicissitudes.

†

An hour later Professor Lacombe and FB had moved to the dining room and, over oysters followed by seafood cassoulet, Lacombe began elaborating further on the more general history of dune stabilisation, augmenting what he had been able to illustrate about the movement of the sands with the help of the morphological charts and the living view out the window.

'It concerns both land and sea,' said Lacombe. 'Houses that have been buried by the creeping giant that is the Dune du Pyla, land that has been colonised by westerly winds full of sand, and channels that must remain navigable for the families who rely on them for fishing and, these days, for tourism. You will see how, as far back as the 1700s, we have been attempting to control the march of sand in the *bassin*. On Cap Ferret we planted *Ammophila arenaria* as long ago as the 1700s to try to hold the dunes together so the northern channel did not fill up with sand. We laid cypress branches upwind of each planting for the sand to coalesce. I will show you tomorrow. Then we built the Gascony palisades, the slat fences you have already seen pictures of in Paris, and we still do. All this has an effect, but the most effective is the *gourbet*, the marram grasses, the *Ammophila arenaria*. I do believe that without it the charts for 1829, 1912 and so on would be significantly different. How is your cassoulet?'

FB nodded enthusiastically. 'Delicious, thank you.'

†

After dinner they took a glass of cognac on a small open terrace which overlooked the steep hotel garden. Now they were staring directly into the treetops. It was a warm spring evening and Lacombe was in the mood. His high pale forehead shone with the plenitude the Loup Garou was once again offering him. He had a captive audience and as he talked seemed unwilling to notice how increasingly distracted his pupil had become.

'Human beings are quick to forget the conditions which give them their breath of life,' the professor said. 'The *bassin* is a case in point, precisely because the power of nature here resists abstraction. You cannot live here, you cannot work or raise a family on these shores, without taking into account the tides, the winds, the sand. For that reason,' he concluded, 'it is an emblematic environment.'

An emblematic environment. This remark resonated with FB, but not only in the way Lacombe intended. The student took the opportunity to concur emphatically with his mentor, as much to mask his interior excitements as anything else. There had been a long build-up to this trip in their tutorials, Lacombe had been impressed enough by FB's work to deem the excursion warranted, and FB didn't want to let him down.

'Yes, it does seem to be a remarkable area,' FB said. 'And the charts here are such a helpful illustration to have in the field, as it were.'

Lacombe's face grew serious. 'Francis, to transfer this knowledge to your situation in Australia is an opportunity for us both.'

But FB felt far from ambassadorial at that moment. So he simply nodded in a bashful way, and said nothing.

'Tomorrow,' Lacombe continued, 'we will spend the morning at Pyla and the afternoon at Cap Ferret. By the time we are sitting out on this terrace again in the evening you will have learnt as much in twenty-four hours as in the whole time you've been in Paris.'

'Well, I'm grateful,' FB replied. 'Though I feel I've learnt an enormous amount in Paris, and not only through my studies.'

Lacombe nodded. 'There is a fundamental difference between what you can learn here at the *bassin* and the events you have been involved in on the streets of Paris. You know the slogan I saw written on a wall before we left? *Sous les pavés, la plage.*'

Once again the professor had his student's full attention.

Sous les pavés, la plage. Under the cobblestones lies the beach.

†

Cycling back to the mill in the dusk, tears began to fall down FB's cheeks in the most unexpected way. Was it all too much, this quickening convergence of his heart and mind? Perhaps. Was he suddenly homesick for the astringent and slightly defensive version of existence which he led in Australia? Taking his mother-made sandwiches to work every day, putting up with her moral frown, her loving control, and also the mediocrity of Gibbon and co. at the CRB. Even his involvement in the Moorabool Chamber Orchestra was only half satisfactory, what with the slipping tempos and the off notes. He had made do but had always longed for the kind of fullness he was now experiencing. Professor Lacombe at the top of his game. Mathilde, in her own magnetic way, at the top of hers. So why the tears?

As he cycled through the curling avenue of pines which led him back from Arcachon through Anguillon to the port of La Teste he saw how the boats previously marooned at their moorings were now being floated once again by the incoming tide. He felt as if the tide itself was rushing through his own body, pushing him back towards the salt pastures and Mathilde, flushing out of his heart a complex arterial emotion of saltwater, lust, inspiration and knowledge. Such was this whelming, after the austerity of his former life, that it had to become vocal. He groaned loudly as he pedalled. The tears were simply not enough.

He kept to the shoreline, as Mathilde had instructed,

and by the time he reached the grass path which ran back along the salt pastures to the mill he did actually stop for a moment and gather himself. He couldn't show up in the state he was in.

FB dismounted amongst trees where the path ran north along an embankment which joined a dyke not far from the mill. No-one could see him from there. Breathing loudly now through his mouth he leant the bike against his hip and wiped his face. Then, looking about just to make sure, he pushed the bike in against a tree and pissed into the bushes.

Walking the bike through the trees along the embankment path he heard music up ahead. The sound of a drum kit and bass floated over the salt pastures, also a voice, and strings. It came as a surprise and extracted him from his own whelmings. It was recorded music, and after a few more steps he began to recognise a tune. His face broke into a smile as he realised he knew what it was and also where it must be coming from.

Quickening his pace in a gloaming light which, like the saltwater, seemed to be descending onto the *prés salés,* he began to feel ridiculously light and happy. Suddenly the light became beautiful, the pastures to his left fecund and roseate with the late solar glow. A few minutes more and he felt cleansed, transformed, as if those tears and that groan had been the very last dregs of a former self.

As he moved closer to the mill he was convinced the music was coming from there. The song ended and

the next one began, 'Fixing a Hole'. She was playing
Sgt. Pepper's.

†

In the dark, with only a kerosene lantern on the garden
table, they drank her father's wine and smoked next to the
vegetable patch beside the mill. They ate white asparagus
and Belgian chocolate. They kissed, and kissed again.
Whenever FB queried whether or not they should turn the
music down, or whether her father or mother might want
her to go inside to bed, she just laughed. '*Vous êtes tendu, trop
tendu,*' she would tell him. You are tense, too tense. It was
an admonition he'd carry around for the rest of his days.

'My parents have always wanted to be free,' she told
him. 'Free from the Nazis, from prudery, from the guilt of
colonialism, from de Gaulle's patriarchy, from ignorance,
from too much knowledge. It may surprise you, given all
the books in his house, but I remember my father setting
fire to books right here in the garden when I was a child.
Sartre. The Stalinist. Reaction, and counter-reaction.
He wants to be free, but really he just wants to be real.
Like Maman.'

FB stared at her in the glow of the kerosene lamp on the
table. He felt thrilled by her words, by her lips, the way she
sat, and laughed. Her confidence, her sincerity.

He tried to explain how different life had been for him.
In the past. The past not so much of Sartre or Camus but

of Fletcher Jones suits and St Joseph's. How narrow and shrill his upbringing had been.

'But that is not you,' she said. 'And my parents are not me. Otherwise we would not be sitting here together listening to Ringo's ridiculous voice.'

They laughed, she was keeping it light, ahead of the darkness to come. She drank her father's wine.

13

Tuft and Rib

BEFORE FB HAD GOT BACK TO THE HOUSE THAT NIGHT, Mathilde had had her own turbulent evening, talking with her father in his kitchen.

'Why are you here?'

'I'm not quite sure.'

'This is not just about your generation you know. Have you heard about what is happening in Nantes?'

'I know about that.'

'It is not only about students.'

'Well, talk to Francis – he was handing out leaflets at the Renault factory on Île Seguin.'

'Was he?'

'Yes.'

'Then I will talk to him; I immediately liked him. Why weren't you there?'

There was silence for a time. Mathilde pictured herself back in her apartment, with her Coca-Cola and Nathalie Sarraute. It wasn't the only reason, but she didn't want to talk about her period with her father. And anyway, as she told FB, if a book existed on the great things women had achieved while they had their periods her father was sure to know about it. He would thrust it before her.

'I don't know,' was all she said.

'You should.'

'Well, maybe that's why I am here.'

'What do you mean?'

'I'm not sure.'

'So this is where you come when you're not sure.'

'Is that a crime?'

'Look, my dear, you are an adult now. To leave is to collaborate.'

'This is not 1943.'

'Thank God.'

There was another pause, until Mathilde made as if to leave. Her father raised his hand, motioning her to stay. She sat.

'So then, you are an émigré,' he said in English. 'To your own home.'

She shook her head. 'It seems you don't understand,' she said.

'Either that, or you are confused.'

'I am. But still you don't understand. How can you? It's 1968 and you live here in this backwater.'

†

Alain Soubret was offended by Mathilde's implication that his life was no longer relevant to contemporary politics but, as fathers do with their daughters, he laughed it off. She had got up from the table, kissed him on both cheeks and left the house. So while FB had been inspecting the morphological charts of the Bassin d'Arcachon with a glass of orange wine in his hand, she was sitting alone on the shore by the oyster sheds just north of the mill, smoking, thinking.

She respected no-one more than her father and it hurt her deeply when he disapproved of her actions. Part of that respect was due to the personal liberty he had always given her, and how he had fought on her behalf when her mother wanted to curtail her freedoms and have her live a more traditional, even Catholic, life. But she had also travelled the coast and up through the Médoc into Brittany with her father when she was a girl, visiting his old compatriots from the days of the Resistance. She had picked up on what those people shared, the depth of their bond and how it was born out of what was good and right, out of risk and sacrifice. Every one of them had risked their life on more than one occasion. And so, when her father accused her of *collaboration*, it had stung. Her response was to lash out.

There was honesty also in what she had said to her father. There *was* something different about what was going on this time, she just couldn't quite articulate what it was. From my own distance, this far away and all these years

175

later, it would seem to have something to do with irony. Something to do with theatre, imitation, with a sense of everything just going through the motions. Something also to do with mindlessness, with boredom and the mob. Hadn't this whole story been told before, wasn't it always the same?

I imagine Mathilde looking down at the gnarled and brindled oyster shells scattered at her feet, thinking of the way they clung for dear life to the structures the farmers created for them. Did the fierceness of that adhesion strike her then for the first time? The structures that gave the oysters life also killed them. Yet their grip on the structures was more powerful than the tides. What gave them this intensity? It wasn't loyalty, and it had nothing to do with courage. She wouldn't have even been sure if she could attribute it to *instinct*. It just was.

And so perhaps the domination of the state *just was*, the structured hierarchy of the university *just was*, the domination of Renault over their workers *just was*, the certitude of de Gaulle *just was*. Was it possible to break their grip? Would she be working with, or against, the tide if she turned away and didn't even try?

She knew that in her father's world this question was impossible. She knew without doubt that his political stance was as imperviously powerful as the grip of the oysters. And that she was weaker.

14

Time Heaped:
The Organic Hourglass

MATHILDE AND FB PLAYED THE ALBUM ALL NIGHT long, also Marie Laforêt. They talked, she told him her thoughts, told him about her talks with her father. They smoked, they ate, they made love. They both had cause for a certain desperation in their lovemaking, and they didn't hold back. There were feelings they could articulate and feelings they couldn't, or wouldn't, find words for. They spoke in both French and English. There were moments when they felt as one, other moments when they were like creatures from entirely alien habitats.

At six o'clock in the morning FB was woken by gunshots. He was alone in the upper storey of the mill. He lay back, disorientated, listening. The shots seemed close, but not too close. They were coming from the *prés salés*.

He looked over to where Mathilde had lain beside him

on the bed. He could still smell her and was glad she'd returned to the main house before the dawn. How could he ever go in for breakfast with her parents after sleeping with her all night?

Making his way downstairs he found the arm of the old gramophone still butting against the end of the record's groove. He gently lifted it back into its cradle. He noticed the gramophone brand – Radio Anjou – and the black Parlophone label of the disc itself. On the table were the remains of the chocolate they'd shared and an empty packet of Marlboros. He made his way over to the tiny washbasin to splash his face.

How he would cope with a full day on the Dune du Pyla and at Cap Ferret with Professor Lacombe after the night he'd had he was not quite sure. Through the fleur-de-lis in the glass of the mill door he could see it was bright, even glorious outside. But he was hungover and sore.

At breakfast inside the house it was explained to FB that the shots he had heard were duck hunters. Over coffee and croissants Alain Soubret was keen to hear what Francis had to say about the events at the Renault factory. FB went back out to the mill to get the leaflet he'd saved concerning the two hundred Algerians killed near the Pont Saint-Michel.

Mathilde sat quietly at the table as her father read the leaflet and passed it to his wife. The mood at the table darkened and Alain wanted to know how Francis had come to be handing out such material. After FB told him about the man who'd appeared out of the crowd, Alain spoke rapidly to his wife and daughter at great length. Eventually he apologised to FB and explained in English that he and his wife had known two of the people who were killed near the bridge. Mathilde's mother nodded gravely.

As FB attempted to express his condolences Alain waved him silent with his hand. Instead he smiled. 'But you must be surprised by what you encountered?' he suggested. 'You were not expecting a revolution when you arrived in Paris.'

FB smiled too, and agreed. But then he asked: 'Do you think this *is* a revolution, Monsieur Soubret? Is that the right word?'

Alain Soubret shook his head slowly. 'I cannot tell,' he said, 'whether everything is changed or nothing at all. But the demonstrations are now spreading. Even to Bordeaux, I think. And so, the next few days will reveal to us what France, at this moment, is capable of. For certain there are a lot of changes that need to take place. There is a lot of unhappiness. The fact that students and workers have come together to create a pause is, in itself, remarkable. What happens from here will depend on the force of the government, the strategy they adopt.'

'And what do you think they will do, Papa?' asked Mathilde.

Alain thought for a moment, then turned to his wife. 'Madeleine?' he said.

Madeleine Soubret smiled at FB. It was the first time he'd seen her smile and he was struck by how alike she and Mathilde were when she did so. 'If they are stupid,' she said, 'which of course they are not, they will continue with the violence, the suppression. If they are clever, they will leave it to the people to exhaust themselves with their own internal fighting. And, as Mathilde has shown, before long the students will want to take their holidays.'

At this Mathilde shot up out of her chair and left the room.

†

On their walk from the Hotel Loup Garou to the Dune du Pyla, Professor Lacombe, in tennis shoes, slacks, sports jacket and yellow tie, explained to Francis Hershell, in Dunlop Volleys, grey Fletcher Jones slacks and white shirt unbuttoned at the collar, how his beloved hotel got its name. By the time they arrived at the *Grande Dune*, less than an hour later, FB's understanding of it had changed once again, and so had the weather.

They walked in heavy drops of humid rain as Lacombe explained the myth of the werewolf. The Gascony werewolf, or *loup-garou*, was a blood sucking creature, a vampire no less, who sheds its skin every evening, hiding it under a tree, before taking off on its quest for blood. It flies through the sky, it changes form and sends flames from its armpits that can be seen burning overhead at night.

The *loup-garou* can also reduce itself in size to fit through the slightest crack and can therefore invade homes and especially bedrooms. It does however have one weakness, a fatal obsessive addiction to counting. Thus on occasion, outside the back or front door of old Gascony houses, or indeed of other houses across other regions of France, most of which have a version of the same story, you will see a small pile of sand left there for the *loup-garou* to count. In this way she (and she is almost always depicted as a female) is stymied from entering the house for she is compelled to stop and count the grains of sand before she can continue. Inevitably the counting of grains of sand is never quite conclusive and thus the *loup-garou* is condemned, in her obsessive fashion, to begin counting all over again as soon as she has finished. By this time of course the hours of night have passed and before the sun appears she must return to the tree where she left her skin and assume her relatively benign daylit form as a wolf.

With his black umbrella unfurled, Professor Lacombe led FB through the forest of pines, telling the story of the *loup-garou* in the rain, until just as they caught their first glimpse of the dune towering above them through dripping branches, he declared: 'This, Francis, is the pile of sand nature has left out for the *loup-garou* by the back door of the house of France.'

A minute later they came clear of the dripping trees into a full sky of slow-falling rain. Above them towered the off-white massif of the dune. FB could hardly believe his eyes.

It seemed to reach right to the sky, an enormous anomaly amongst the deep green of the pine-forested Gascony coast.

Professor Lacombe, for once, was silent. From where they stood the sand swept down from its apex, slipping ever inland and quite obviously and gradually swallowing the forest. FB remembered the numbers. In 1855 it was measured at a height of thirty-five metres. It now soared over the basin and forest at a height of nearly one hundred metres. The basic physics were simple. At low tide, sand from the Banc d'Arguin at the mouth of the *bassin* would be blown onto the pile. As the height increased, eventually the angle of the dune's inland face would reach thirty-five degrees, at which point gravity would ensure that sand would slip from the apex down the inland side. And there it would spread like a creature over *les landes*. In this way, if you believed the myth, the *loup-garou* was kept counting.

As the professor and his student began the formidable climb up the inland face of sand the rain began to fall even harder. Lacombe remarked between exhausted breaths that it was good luck because the rain meant they had the dune all to themselves. Otherwise, as he said, the biggest sand dune in Europe would be busy with visitors.

At the summit, neither FB's burning thighs and calves nor his virtually sleepless night could quell his appreciation of the view. They stood on the northern end of the dune, which swept away for three kilometres along the coast towards Bayonne. The penny dropped for the young sand engineer as he looked out to sea and sighted the Banc d'Arguin lying salmon-pink directly across the water. The causal chain was obvious now: first the westerly winds, then the Banc d'Arguin, and finally the *Grande Dune*. It was the largest sand phenomenon FB had ever witnessed and he found its simplicity both inspiring and instructive.

Next to him the professor was beaming under his umbrella, lost in who knew how many layers of his erudition. 'It has grown since I was last here,' he told FB enthusiastically. 'It is most certainly wider at the forest side, and seems taller also.'

FB nodded, his mind fascinated by the clear delineations of the mechanism of wind, ocean and sand. He thought of the Bordeaux family he'd read about who had built a villa in the forest back in 1928. By 1936 the house had disappeared beneath the sand. And yet petrified forest fossils had also been found within the dune, indicating that there was a long geologic cycle to it all, a cycle of green growth then sand accretion which further contextualised the dune's current growth phase and, of course, connected to the charts of the *bassin's* morphology he had viewed in the hotel.

There was such a thing as terra firma, FB thought, but this wasn't it. There was no such thing at the Bassin d'Arcachon, where the whole environment was moving about like a jellyfish. One thing, though, he felt was certain: it was a case of the ocean shaping the land rather than the other way around.

Together Professor Lacombe and FB walked slowly south along the ridge of the enormous dune. It was enough to see it to know it was like an unstoppable forest-eating maw in its current phase. And so, in the face of the Dune du Pyla, the engineer must observe and learn, rather than intervene. The dune represented an unavoidable example of the scales that had to be worked with. Short of doing something as vainglorious as Hitler when he'd built his Atlantic Wall along the coast, there was nothing to be done now but learn. Even from where they walked along the dune they could see the tormented redundant shards of Hitler's wall lying like beached concrete whales on the shore below. The whole environment was humbling, which was exactly what Professor Lacombe had brought FB there to learn.

'So,' the professor began, taking down his black umbrella as the rain began to clear, 'we cannot build a barrier at the inland side, therefore our only option would be to somehow cover the Banc d'Arguin from exposure to the wind. You can see how discrete the action is; the Banc d'Arguin defines the Pyla so precisely. An aerial photograph shows the dune almost as a perfectly installed, rectangular kerb of sand set down upon the forest.'

'So you'd cover the Banc d'Arguin with a gigantic tarpaulin?'

'Yes, that's the basic concept, except it would take a monomaniac like Hitler to attempt such a thing. It is a sacrilege for an engineer to say this, but you cannot *manage* the environment in this case. Not by controlling it. Rather, like a cyclist on a road full of cars, you must give way. In this instance, at this moment in geological time, we cannot match the power of the ocean. Unlike on the Cap Ferret over there across the water, our processes are of no use. This is nature at work, Francis, power and energy. A great reminder to us all. And it keeps the *loup-garou* at bay.'

An hour later, as they came down off the dune on the ocean side, a group of schoolchildren were taking turns at running down the slope with glee. FB smiled at them. He remembered doing exactly the same thing as a child: at Point Lonsdale, at Breamlea, at Split Point, at Princetown. But none of those dunes were even a tenth as tall as Pyla. Once again he felt overwhelmed. His own little life had been placed in perspective. Everything he had known and loved was better here, bigger, more numerous, more sensuous but, at the same time, as simple and identical as sand.

†

After arriving back at the Hotel Loup Garou Professor Lacombe and FB enjoyed a brief lunch of soup and baguette before walking down the hill from the Ville d'Hiver to the Thiers jetty, from where the ferry would leave for Cap Ferret. The observations they would make that afternoon, of the Gascony palisades and marram grass plantings that were introduced to Cap Ferret in order to stabilise the sandy cape, would have a lasting effect on FB's work for many years to come. It was not lost on him that this dune stabilisation work had begun at Cap Ferret a full half-century before the official white settlement of Australia. On the ferry across he was reminded of Sydney Harbour as he watched the young ferrymen standing with their cigarettes by the resting mooring ropes with the sunshine glittering on the water and the various small fishing and pleasure craft crisscrossing the lambent stretches amongst the swirl of currents.

Halfway across the *bassin*, Professor Lacombe fell into excited conversation with the person sitting next to them on the bench in the stern. Lacombe was interrogating this Cap Ferret local on the state of the oyster fishery and the attitude of the residents to the various proposed developments on the cape. As a result, FB was free to stare out across the water and let his mind roam.

When he reflects on this ferry ride in his journal it is most certainly she, and not so much the technology of the dune work at Pyla or Cap Ferret, that preoccupies him. He visualises her coming past the ferry in her *pinasse*, waving at him from the sunlit tiller. He keeps his eyes peeled in case she does in fact sail by. This was an impossible daydream, if for no other reason than that the weather was cloudy, almost humid. He writes of longing for the evening even as he is enjoying the work of the day – a perfect situation, one has to admit – and goes so far as to wonder if she'd ever be content to settle with him somewhere on the ocean shores of the *bassin*. '*Paris seems a long way away,*' he writes, '*and Geelong might as well be Jupiter. M is so attractive I can barely stand it, and Prof L seems to have a broader understanding of the dunes than I ever imagined.*'

They docked at Cap Ferret and were met by Pierre Green, an Anglo-Frenchman working full time on Cap Ferret overseeing the ongoing stabilisation work. He was a well-built man with a hawk-like countenance not dissimilar to that of Alain Soubret. He wore shorts, FB noted, the first time he'd seen a Frenchman do so, even in the hottest weather. '*It must be the English in him,*' FB wrote.

FB also remarked, in a suddenly impersonal tone: '*Pierre Green drove Professor Lacombe and the Australian student Francis Herschell out to the tip of the cape in his blue Renault Ondine sedan.*' This was, of course, the same model of car FB drove in later years and which made him such an easily recognisable figure around Geelong and the Great Ocean Road.

Out on the tip of the cape a spring wind was blowing, tousling the strands of the marram grass plantings and thrumming through the revolutionary slat-fence palisades. These were the apparatus that Lacombe had brought FB to see. Unlike on the Pyla side, where the pines had been planted over two hundred kilometres of coastline in order to stop the marching dunes and to turn the salt pastures of *les landes* into something productive, this was dune work on a smaller, more local scale.

They walked the low dunes, shielding their eyes from the glare off the water. As they walked, Pierre Green described how the work was helping to keep the north channel through the passes open. Looking out to the passes FB could see the Dune de Pyla in the distance on the far side, and the scudding Atlantic pressing itself through the mouth of the bay in between. The hydraulic pressure of the ocean current was obviously immense, so that the cape would easily be torn and eroded without the engineering efforts. Behind them, less than a kilometre back from the southern tip, the Cap Ferret lighthouse stood sentinel over the wearback of the waves.

'Unlike over at Pyla, it is possible for our work to be effective here,' Lacombe explained. 'There is of course a human community in the dunes of Ferret that stretches right along the peninsula. Some of these families have lived here for hundreds of years and would like to carry on doing so. Thus, that is one of our criteria. When the first stabilisation methods were deemed effective so long ago, not in making the land productive but simply in stabilising the cape formation, they were continued. Whether or not they are applicable to your situation in Australia I don't know, but I see no real reason why they wouldn't be. Depending, of course, on your anemometer data and the PH values of the sand. But from what you have described – low-lying hummocks, parabolic dunes, occasional Aeolian formations, in a wind-intensive onshore situation – what you are seeing here could be of some value.'

So this was the very hour on Cap Ferret that confirmed the migration of an idea. Together the three men walked the dunes of the cape, Pierre Green and Professor Lacombe pointing out to FB the way in which the marram grass plantings (they used the local word *gourbet*) were staggered, and how each palisade, once the sand had built up and was beginning to cover it, had another identical palisade built straight on top of the sand it had accumulated. And so on and so on. It was also pointed out again how something as simple as laying pine branches downwind of these palisades can have a remarkable effect in the coalescing of the sand.

FB assured his mentors that it was all very instructive and that, from his point of view, he couldn't see any reason why the Cap Ferret methods wouldn't be transferrable to the Victorian coast. And so an air of concord and enthusiasm seemed to permeate the resinous air. All the while, however, FB's heart was beating fast, as the talk of what could or could not be applied back home in Victoria forced him to simultaneously reflect on the implications of the deeper desires that had gripped him. The emotional truth was in direct contradiction to his encouraging comments about the science and engineering of the sand. He had no desire at all to return and apply his findings at home. Even as he heard the words coming from his mouth about the specific compatibility of the Gascony palisades to his home coast he felt he was speaking in bad faith. He would have preferred a job as Pierre Green's morphological assistant right there on the Cap Ferret hummocks than a quasi-triumphant return to the CRB in Geelong with the solution to their problems. The last few days had changed everything. He did not care any longer about the conundrum of the kangaroo down the hole, let alone Gibbon's shoddiness when it came to reducing the drift at Eastern View or on the Bluff Road behind Barwon Heads, but here he was pretending that he did. Perhaps Pierre Green, having just met the young antipodean engineer, could sense a certain ambivalence in his reactions, but he felt sure that Lacombe hadn't.

Quickly then, as the minutes, then the quarter-hours, the half-hours then the whole afternoon passed on the dunes and up in the lighthouse at Cap Ferret, the sense of happiness and relief FB had felt at the Dune du Pyla deteriorated into anxiety and confusion. He maintained a polite demeanour and, oddly enough, his conversational French that afternoon, perhaps due to this feeling of being only half present in his words, was as fluent as it had ever been. But inside, in a realm beyond translation, he felt mercurial and stricken, as confused and torn as the currents rushing past them directly out from the shore.

15

Scoured

THE YOUNG LOVERS' LAST NIGHT TOGETHER WAS HARDLY an idyll and yet the gravity and tension of those hours only deepened their passion and left it etched indelibly in FB's mind. Once the inspection of the dunes at Cap Ferret was over, and after enjoying a Perrier on Pierre Green's back terrace near the lighthouse, Lacombe and FB returned on the ferry to Arcachon, disembarking at the Thiers jetty and walking through the level streets of the town and then up the slope back to the Hotel Loup Garou. Lacombe seemed still oblivious to FB's internal turmoil and for this the young engineer was grateful. They talked as they walked, first about the enormous remnants of the Atlantic Wall they'd seen on the beach at Cap Ferret, then about the captivity Lacombe and his friend Louis Poirier had endured after being captured at Dunkirk during the war. FB had noticed graffiti on the concrete *blockhaus* shards of the wall on the beach, which reminded him immediately of Paris. He commented to Lacombe on how a once-functional infrastructure can be overturned into an expressive rebellion directly against its intended use. The angular wedges of *blockhaus* carried mostly inane slogans to do with soccer players, but they were nevertheless, in their own way, inscriptions serving as declarations of freedom. Lacombe found this observation interesting and gave Francis a look that suggested he may have just intuited that there was more to this young Australian than his professional interest in sand. And then he said, perhaps pointedly, in French:

'C'est intéressant ce que vous dites Francis, mais en même temps nous ne devons pas prétendre que nous pouvons nous libérer de la nature. Au contraire, nous devons travailler avec elle. La liberté aux dépens de la terre ne vaut pas la peine d'être considérée.'

When they arrived back to the hotel Lacombe seemed invigorated, not at all tired from their long day in the field. He insisted that he drive Francis out to Mathilde's home in La Teste. When FB protested that he had his bicycle with him Lacombe went straight to the bike, picked it up with great gusto and wedged it into the back seat of his car with one wheel poking out. Then the professor got behind the wheel and there was nothing FB could do but comply. They set off for La Teste-de-Buch.

†

Earlier in the day, when Mathilde had sat beside her father on the sofa to discuss her situation some more, Alain had asked her about Professor Lacombe and what he was teaching Francis. Mathilde had told her father that she found the professor very progressive and even wise in his opinions but that his personality was stuck in the past. 'He is teaching Francis about how things accumulate,' she said. 'And how things that might appear to be the strongest facts of the earth are finally, in geological time, whittled away.'

'He is teaching the revolution then, is he not?'

'Perhaps, but a very slow one.'

So it was that when Lacombe and FB arrived at the Soubret house at approximately six o'clock that evening Alain Soubret was pleasantly surprised. He eagerly invited the professor to stay for a glass of wine.

Mathilde and FB also took a glass of wine and sat with Alain and Lacombe beside the fig tree in the garden between the main house and the *moulin*. Lacombe was at his most relaxed and responded happily when Alain Soubret began to recount what Mathilde had described to him of the work he was involved in. When Alain went so far as to reiterate his analogy between the accumulation of sand, the principles of geological accretion and wearback, and revolution, Lacombe seemed both amused and delighted. And in response he immediately emphasised the importance of a slowing-down of human activity which Mathilde herself had touched on in her discussion with Alain earlier in the day.

'The dune world is a civilisation in itself,' Lacombe told them, as light dappled by the large leaves of the fig tree played on his face. 'Though admittedly its main inhabitants are meiofauna, tiny creatures that thrive on the organic debris amongst sand. Years of observing these creatures, and their interaction with the sand environment, has possibly affected my view of human society and politics. Under the influence of all this, I believe that what is needed most now is a more profound human revolution than we are currently seeing. What is required is a patient revolution, a long view, a recalibration of our society to the pace of the earth's workings, to the speed of the wheel of time, the way a bird waits in a tree.'

Alain Soubret nodded thoughtfully, listening to this eminent Parisian with genuine appreciation.

'Patience,' Lacombe continued, 'but not *complaisance*, or submission to those who do otherwise. As you well know, in the years of the Nazi occupation such a balance was required, between patience and commitment. It is required now too. Always, in fact. We must shun the drama of the cultural avalanche, the blinding dazzle of the spectacle, and recommit to the slow realities of earth, the accumulation, rather than the sudden outbreak, of life's meaning. Otherwise all this momentum, this supposed fecundity that has taken over France in the last few days, will take its place in historical time as a momentary and rather pointless paroxysm – and an illusory one at that.'

Alain Soubret nodded again, then raised his finger to interrupt the professor's flow.

'Professor, if I may. What do you mean, exactly, when you suggest that we move in step with the earth? Are you, for instance, recommending a return to bows and arrows, to walking the *prés salés* on stilts? How will this work on a day-to-day basis?'

Lacombe smiled at his host, who likewise smiled in return. FB observed in his journal that the two older men were like a pair of hungry insects happy to feed off each other.

The professor sipped his wine. 'It means a reordering of priorities *in the mind*,' he said. 'So that we understand the exact possibilities of our participation. Our role in the accumulation.'

Alain Soubret now laughed a little, as if questioning the professor's rather abstract language. 'I said "in reality", Professor, on a day-to-day level.'

Lacombe returned his glass to the garden table. His face became serious. 'Well,' he began, 'there are many mechanisms to undo, or even replace, but really what I mean is that society needs to reconfigure itself *metaphysically*. We need to re-embrace the natural world, not as a holiday from reality but, well, as our only true guide and teacher.'

Alain laughed more expressively now, and affectionately. 'Yes, yes,' he said, 'but what about *here and now, on a day-to-day level*, Professor?'

Now Lacombe also smiled. 'The concepts of *here* and *now* to which you refer are in fact more accurately described as *space* and *time*, possibly the most theoretical concepts of them all!'

'Yet they are also the most real . . .' replied Alain, raising his wine to his lips, while simultaneously pushing a small ceramic dish of walnuts towards Lacombe.

Mathilde and FB were listening attentively, sitting side by side across the broad green table.

Alain Soubret went on '. . . the most real concepts, yes, the most affecting in the heart too. Space, for instance, is our physical home, and time is memory, exile, forgetting.'

Lacombe nodded, as if to say 'of course'. When pressed, however, he refused to outline precise programmatic solutions for the problems of urban modernity, preferring instead to state that as far as he was concerned the students in Paris were acting from a pastoral impulse, without even knowing it.

At this Mathilde shifted in her seat.

'It's true, I think,' Lacombe said, addressing the daughter now and not the father. 'But you must remember that landscape, the *paysage*, is not in itself a festival. Life, in fact, is not a festival. This impulse to disturb the grid of the cobblestones in Paris for something organic is the correct one, but only as long as it is understood that a life lived with nature, with soil, sand, wind, stone, sky and water, requires more patience and deeper discipline than a life of urban abstraction.'

Mathilde looked glum now. 'This is something I think about,' she said quietly.

'Let us take insecticides as an example,' Lacombe went on. 'The farmers spray their crops for short-term gain while at the same time removing the very forms of life that will sustain us in the end. They have removed small risks but created a much bigger one. It is all very well to say that the CRS are barbarians for spraying their citizens as if they too are pests, but the farmer that is killing nature is often held up as the very essence of France!'

Alain Soubret shifted in his seat, growing impatient now. He was glad Madame Soubret was down at the port helping to size the oysters. She would most certainly have objected to this academic from Paris lecturing them in a most undialectical fashion about the so-called 'realities' of living with nature.

At the time FB was surprised that Mathilde did not challenge Lacombe more directly – not his views, but the pedagogical way in which he delivered them. Yet despite the events in Paris, one thing he had learnt about the French since he'd arrived was their intrinsic respect for process and comportment. It was one thing to stand with the gang at the barricades hurling refuse at the police, but quite another to criticise a professor to his face. Especially not in your father's garden.

It was Alain who spoke next, and quite firmly, in keeping with how he had been with Mathilde since she'd arrived home.

'Professor, I find your ideas interesting, and there is much to like about them, but with due respect, they are also about as light and loose as the sand you have been working on for so many years. I would suggest that what you call "nature" is, frankly, never divisible from culture, certainly not from our human subjectivity. Your plantings and palisades, your *gourbet* barricades, *are* culture. They will not, however, solve the problems at Renault, at Citroën, or at the Rhodiaceta plant, nor will they humanise Papon and his thugs. What will bind the students and workers together will be an urgent sense of human decency. It is always a cultural issue, not one of nature.'

Lacombe's back straightened a little but he nodded slowly. Then, opening his arms wide and gesturing at the fig canopy dappling them all, he said, 'Yet here we are!'

†

Later that evening, when Mathilde and FB were walking through the *prés salés* in the moonlight on their way to the water, FB suggested to her that her position was somewhere halfway between that of her father's and Lacombe's.

'Perhaps you are right,' she said. 'It is I who am blown by the wind. First here, then there. It is exhausting. I envy them both their certitude, their stability. I am not stable.'

It was true. She had torn up the steel fasteners at the base of the plane trees of Saint-Michel with her own hands, she had roared and chanted, she had hurled not only cobblestones but glass bottles, broken and jagged, at the enemy. Yet she had still felt the need to retreat to the Rue des Quatre-Vents, to the Galerie Sarcon, to the sanctuary not of political ethics but of Mondrian's dunes. Back and forth she had gone over those few days, needing one thing just as much as the other. The urgency of the real, the truth of the imagined. Timelessness, and time.

†

Although Professor Lacombe had only stayed at the Soubret house for a little over an hour, it was a visit that would long be remembered. When he had left, with polite farewells from Alain and Mathilde and a commitment from FB to meet him for lunch the next day at the Loup Garou, FB was invited to dine with Mathilde's parents. He accepted.

Over dinner he was asked to tell them about Australia, its politics, its culture, its treatments of the Aborigines, whom Alain had read about the year before when they were finally given the right to vote. FB was asked to describe the culture of Australian cities, their demographics, architecture, landscape, literature and music. Then, after the meal, FB was given a tour of Alain's bookshelves. Once again, though, as amongst the low hummocks at Cap Ferret, he was distracted. As Alain Soubret expressed his preference for Montaigne – *un garçon local* – but then grew discursive about Frantz Fanon's sanctioning of violence, FB could manage no stimulating response. This was partly because of language difficulties, partly because his private turmoil was now silting up any fluency he had attained, but looking back he also felt he had *'behaved as dully as a dutiful schoolboy'*. It is possible that Alain Soubret did not expect much more from his Australian visitor, distracted as he was himself not only by the conversation he had had with Professor Lacombe but by the arguments with his daughter and the ongoing tension such conflict was causing between himself and his wife. Earlier in the day, while FB was off on the dunes with Lacombe, and Alain and Mathilde had sparred, Madame Soubret had scolded her husband for being so eager to risk his daughter's safety. The whole little family had exploded. Madame Soubret had stormed off, hence her absence during Lacombe's visit. What FB and the professor had walked into on their return from Cap Ferret was the smouldering aftermath. FB had noticed straightaway that Mathilde seemed sad and distant. They'd kissed briefly, but in front of her father and Lacombe he found this unbearable. As Alain and Lacombe were taking their seats at the garden table, Mathilde and FB had gone alone to the kitchen together to fetch the drinks and walnuts. She asked him how it had gone with Lacombe and he replied that it was both good and bad. 'Pyla is a monster,' she had said then. 'It can never be satisfied.'

As she'd brusquely picked up the tray and begun to move towards the garden, FB had said, to try to lighten the mood: 'Yeah, I prefer the Mondrians.'

A smile had briefly come into her eyes.

†

When Madame Soubret had returned in time for dinner she was loving towards Mathilde but perfunctory with her husband and also with FB. Over the meal she seemed to relax a bit, as the young Australian's exotic tales from the southern hemisphere distracted her from their disagreements, but when Alain and FB got up to look at the bookshelves FB noticed how she immediately turned to Mathilde with a look of fond distress.

The mother knew better than the father, and certainly better than FB, the decision the daughter would make. She was already grieving, even before her daughter had uttered it.

When the tour of the bookshelves and coffee was over, FB excused himself in order to return to his lodgings in the mill to write up his notes. What, we might wonder, could he possibly write of sand and dunes, of slat fences, palisades and marram grass, when so much was going on inside his heart?

He sat downstairs instead by the cold stove, his blank page lit by the kerosene lamp. He smoked. He waited for her to arrive.

†

When she did eventually arrive it was almost midnight. She found him cheek down on the pages of his writing, the lamp wick low, the mill bitterly cold. What had been heavy-humid rain earlier in the day had now thinned and freshened. The drama had begun to appear in the sky. Brief ziggurats of lightning could be seen out over the *prés salés* and the passes towards Cap Ferret. A wind had picked up, too, in the marine dark the rain was silver and intermittent.

She had come to tell him she was catching the train to Bordeaux in the morning. She was returning to Paris. She would say he had a special place in her heart, a natural connection to her deepest self, but their paths must diverge. They each had to be comfortable in their own skin, he amongst the dunes in Australia, she in Rue Monge, helping to ensure that this progress was not squandered.

For Mathilde, raised as her father's daughter, the world was political, be it in the streets of Paris or in the farmhouses of Gascony. It seemed that only the *bassin* was the exception, the wild seaway that gave her, and her father, their *situation originelle*. But life had to evolve, to be lived, one could not simply stay rooted at the source. If so, the source itself may become fettered, entangled, dire.

For FB, however, the landscape had little to do with politics at all. He was not driven along his childhood coast visiting heroes of a resistance. Instead he was part of an invading force, marched off to mass, drilled in the catechism and presented with his books and violin as a trophy-child to the rest of the extended family. Dunes were for running down rather than allegories, and the sea itself was an ever-sibilant stranger.

He lay sleeping on the record he had inscribed in his own blank page. Dreaming of her. His dream come true. The passage on the page was the description of his imagined sighting of her from the ferry. Coming by in her *pinasse*. At one with her world: the sparkling glare, the turquoise sheet of water beneath her, shifting this way then that.

But now the water was dark in the reaches between streaks of lightning, waiting beyond the steady quiet of the *prés salés*.

†

She was crying as she lit the stove, knowing that decisions like the one she had made deny entire worlds. Her heart was rent, like in a nineteenth-century novel. But back then, when such novels were being written by the likes of Balzac, Zola, Hugo and Flaubert, the local people around La Teste-de-Buch and Arcachon were walking across the squelching marshes on stilts. She had been born too late for that but nevertheless had been taught how to light a fire, to handle a *pinasse*, to fight for justice. She had always wanted that honour, that dignity, but it did not lie for her in remote parts of the coast as it once had.

She touched his arm. He became aware of her now. He stared as she joggled the coals with the fire tongs.

As she turned from the glow the rain weakened outside. Her freckles were golden, flickering, framed by the open door of the stove. He did not think of these golden freckles as grains of sand but, in different circumstances, in a more distant and luxurious mood, he might have.

'*J'y vais, Francis,*' she said. '*Retour á Paris.*'

✝

Sometimes, in the years afterwards, when he was reading a book and marvelling at how *geological* words were, how they contained whole strata of emotion which depended on the way they were said, or when they were said, he thought of those words Mathilde uttered by the stove as he was emerging from his dream. He knew what they meant, in a way that went well beyond the details of the La Teste railway timetable.

'I'm going, Francis. Back to Paris.'

Six words that could have been said in any number of happier, or more ordinary situations. Six words only, but in this case FB knew straightaway that the meaning of those six words transcended their literal meaning. This transcendence was akin to the difference between a map and its landscape. One gave the literal facts, the other contained emotional infinitudes.

It was as if he had known those six words were coming, and had already thought a lot about them before they arrived. She had never, after all, pretended that she was not conflicted.

So when he replied, 'I'll come with you,' it was already in a crestfallen voice that would return in his nightmares for decades. Why was it he who was doomed to represent the politics of nostalgia, a retreat from the real and the truth? Was it something about him, or something about where he was from? In a congested urban world where a life lived with nature is nearly impossible, a desire to do so can appear fey, childlike, stupid, or even insane. Yet he had known when they stood together by the black telephone in Saint-Sulpice that Mathilde understood that insanity. Understood it, yes, but with those six words in the mill she confirmed her conclusion that such madness was irrelevant in the struggle for a better world.

They boiled the iron kettle on the stovetop and in silence drank black Darjeeling from the tin he'd brought all the way from home. Outside in the night the Atlantic breathed its ancient breath against the handmade window-panes of the mill.

16

Grain by Grain

EVERYWHERE, PEPPERED AMONGST EVEN THE MOST technical sections of FB's papers, are small aperçus, aphorisms and general quotes he has written down. These lines, thoughts, reflections, derived largely from his reading, make obvious the deeper resonance he brought to bear upon his technical work. There is a life in his archive which one could describe as philosophical, even poetic at times, as intricate wind-vector diagrams and hard observational graphs on sand drift are annotated with the thoughts of Baudelaire or Guillevic, Hélène Cixous or Guy Debord. No matter how humdrum or perfunctory his fieldwork had necessarily to be, it became clear to me, by what I saw in its margins, that a thinking heart was always present in the tasks. There would therefore be no way of eviscerating the emotion and feeling from this scientist, this civil engineer. Nor from his sand archive.

If you follow nature, you have to accept whatever is capricious and twisted in nature.

Piet Mondrian

Autrement – 'otherly'

Now, of the music summoned by the birth
That separates us from the wind and sea

Wallace Stevens

He was now more than ever determined to make his life an unbroken echo of what he had perceived when he was young and to teach other men in poetry what he had learned in sorrow.

Halldór Laxness

So that the loss itself is not lost . . .

Dune 42 in Area 16 was extensively reshaped to a profile based upon that of the artificial littoral dune which exists along the French coast south of Bordeaux

The earth, the earth does not lie.

Patrick Modiano, *La Place de l'étoile*

I have been looking on these layered 'archaeologies', these gold and red piles of different histories and systems as a metaphor for the human psyche; the way each of us could be seen as a walking many-layered world of passions, ancestral memories, neuroses, genetic patterns and ancient archetypes.

John Wolseley

Sartre preferred food that had been transformed to disguise its natural origins. Raw vegetables were 'too natural', but okay 'after human intervention transforms them into a puree.' Cakes and pastries were ideal because they had 'been thought out by man and made on purpose.'

Bill McCormick quoting from
Stuart Zane Charme on Sartre

clastic/clast – from Greek klastos: broken in pieces

†

Once he'd returned to Paris at the end of May he set out immediately for the metro to find Mathilde. Paris was a different city now; the temper had passed, order had been restored to the streets and the bus timetable. Only occasionally could a stray cobble be seen, a rough hemisphere of stones still disassembled. De Gaulle had called elections for the last week of June. Commerce had resumed, though now with hopes for a pay rise in the pressured hearts of workers. The scholars resumed study for their exams, just as on the heights of the Pyrenees wind and gravitational impulses ground the edifices of the earth into tiny airborne grains destined for swirling sorrel streams which would ultimately find their way to the Atlantic coast.

He had caught the metro as far as Cluny – La Sorbonne then walked. A block north of Mathilde's apartment building he took a breath over a cup of tea in a brasserie. He noted the subsidence of urgency in the air on Saint-Germain, then too as he crossed the market stalls and passed into Rue Monge. He felt this change of air as an awful vanishing, an inexplicable disappearance, as if he were missing a limb. This is a common enough metaphor for the pain of unrequited or disappearing love. A re-ignition of the city's revolution was not, after all, what he was committed to.

Stirring the tea he had a familiar feeling, but one that lessened over the weeks and months: he felt *too Australian.* With Mathilde, during those final hours before they had left the city, it had been possible to have fun with this hick-ish feeling. She had accepted him, he knew that, and he was also prepared to believe that she even loved him. He felt he carried something of the tides and their reality with him and then, at the Cap Ferret lighthouse, high up with the Fresnel lens as Pierre Green showed them the bird's-eye view over the dunes of the Bassin d'Arcachon, he felt somehow deeply native to the subject of their interest. The knowledge of sand and shore was a universal language, and he felt he was gathering a fluent tongue. But now, back in the city where such littoral openings could be found only in the imagination, and with the awful and pathetic loneliness of his rejection somehow exposed by the light pouring into the broad boulevard, he felt an acid emptiness, as if his own better self had been gnarled by the dry horizontality of the land from which he came.

Mathilde's apartment at 40 Rue Monge was across the street and some hundred metres further along from the brasserie. He was close, but the closer he got the stranger he became. His self-consciousness tightened, the repressions of his plain and conservative upbringing re-gripped him. His tea grew cold.

Approaching Mathilde's building soon afterwards he realised he didn't have the code to open the door to the street. Above him the sky seemed to darken with the utter haplessness of this realisation, as if a southern crag had leant in over Paris to frown at him.

It began to rain. He crossed back over Rue Monge and waited under the burgundy awning of a florist. He knew nothing of what her movements would be, the rhythm of her days, and yet his only hope was to intercept her. But how, in all that time, and all that space?

After an hour in the cold, with the colour of the awning gradually deepening with the rain, he felt entirely bereft. He could not stand the situation any longer, and strode away in the direction of the Boulevard Saint-Germain.

In Rue des Quatre-Vents a half-hour later he found the Galerie Sarcon closed. There was no reason for her to be there – he knew that the Mondrian exhibition was now over – unless of course she was hoping to see him.

Under the cobblestone lies . . .

†

The aperçus and aphorisms in the margins of his charts, diagrams and calculations, along with the things that simply occurred to him as he went along (such as the fact that the dune situation of Cap Ferret could almost be transferrable to those Mondrian painted at Domburg) began to form a telling relationship with the main body of his technical research as I explored the archive.

> *Data obtained at Blakeney in Norfolk by the writer showed that the first 7cms of a dune soil contained b/w 1184 and 8032 rabbit droppings per sq mtr, but in fact, although this appears large, it only represents an annual addition of about 0.18% by weight to the soil. More significant is the fact that these rabbit droppings decay very slowly and represent localised centres of high water-retaining capacity into which the roots penetrate and are especially exploited by them.*
>
> Edward Salisbury, *Downs and Dunes*

> *Apollo had granted him the gift of understanding nature's voices and likewise of realising when speech was pointless.*
>
> Roberto Calasso

After a time, the two components, the cultural reflections and the geomorphological statistics, began to seem themselves like the ocean and shore. But was it the objective coolness of the dune-form analyses, the sand-drift graphs and the wind-vector diagrams that were the ocean, or was the ocean best represented by the sad wisdoms of Camus as he tried to negotiate a path of dignity inside the mess that was French colonialism?

For us, it is clear that the only nationalism at issue here is the nationalism of sunshine.

Albert Camus

And was it the accumulative effect of FB's sand-themed metaphors that best represented the beach and hummocky dunes, or was this better expressed by the cumulative piles of statistics resulting from the persistence of his daily observations? I remembered FB laughing in the bookshop one day as he suggested, rather enigmatically, that if you swapped *space* for *time* the work of some writers was like a king tide that encompassed and flooded a whole era. He said Proust was one such writer. In England, he believed, Virginia Woolf was too. And Joyce in Ireland. I mention this to demonstrate that he was not above (or below) employing the analogy of the tides even in conversation. When you spend your life inspecting the zone between the tides, or merely inspecting the inspections, as I have been doing, the constant roll and lunar cycle of ebb and flow which is the signature of the territory becomes in itself a way of seeing the world. For instance, I know surfers who argue that the dynamic beach breaks on the Atlantic coast of France create a different type of person to the long swelling incubations we endure here along the Great Ocean Road. This is ethnological, of course, the species *as* environment, but it applies – whether it be to the civil engineer, the writer or surfer. Or the lover, for that matter.

Thus Mathilde's disappearance is everywhere underneath FB's papers from 1968 on.

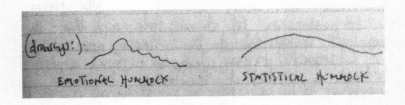

†

In the three weeks between his arrival back in Paris and the French elections of 23 and 30 June, FB struggled with the polarity of Professor Lacombe's renewed enthusiasm for the internationalisation of his dune research and his own feelings of disorientation at walking the streets of the city without Mathilde. Like a tourist of his own heart's geography, he visited Saint-Sulpice, the Galerie Sarcon, even the *tabac* at Clamart where they had opened the door for the bird in the cage. At Saint-Sulpice he found no black telephone on a tree stump but rather the tidied grey *place* ringed with green buses and grey pigeons. The stump itself had been removed. At the Galerie Sarcon he found the dunes of Mondrian replaced with the self-portraits of an Alsatian painter, Gilles Clairvaux. Although he liked Clairvaux's gentle pictures, they made no real impression on him at all. How could they? Likewise, FB himself seemed to have made little impression on the city; he was not recognised at the gallery nor, of course, at the Clamart *tabac*, where he bought a pack of Gauloises to the haunting tune of the canary's trill. The singing bird clashed with the deathly silence in his heart. It grated and he rushed out of the shop so abruptly that he nearly knocked over an old Spaniard with a walking stick who was coming to buy his daily paper. FB apologised profusely in English, his French momentarily deserting him. The Spaniard was taken aback and quite obviously annoyed.

He also walked all the way along the Boulevard Saint-Michel to Place Denfert-Rochereau, completing the course of the 13 May march which he had abandoned on the Pont Saint-Michel. He doesn't say so in his diaries, but perhaps he felt that if he finally completed the route of the demonstration his fate would somehow be redeemed and Mathilde would appear, walking across the hemi-stitch of the cobbles, a book under her arm, a smile on her lips? It wasn't to be. When he arrived in the wide *place* the traffic seemed coarse and the bustle of the city's inhabitants impervious. He stood for a time as if in an ocean maelstrom, staring at the grandiloquent still point of the grey lion in the heart of the square, before turning left down Boulevard Arago and heading for the river.

On 14 June, after a lonely fortnight of wandering and study, he felt his luck might have changed. While heading out to a lecture at the School of Mines he saw Mathilde's friend Gilles talking with a group of people on the steps of the church at Saint-Germain-des-Prés. He had never been introduced to Gilles but had seen him from a distance with Mathilde on the day that Lacombe and he had picked her up at Rue Monge when they were heading for the dunes. If he had felt a pang of jealousy then, he felt only hope now as suddenly a lifeline appeared between Mathilde's life and his own.

Stopping in his tracks he waited for Gilles and his little group to disperse. Despite the warm summer air it was quiet in the square, with no-one much about. But Gilles and his friends were animated.

Eventually, what FB hoped would happen did, and the two men and one young woman Gilles had been conversing with all kissed him on both cheeks then set off past Les Deux Magots and along Saint-Germain. Gilles, on the other hand, turned right and walked off across the *place* towards the river along Rue Bonaparte – but not before glancing at FB standing alone only twenty metres away. Their eyes met briefly. Before FB could raise a hand to indicate his need to talk, Gilles had hurried off in the other direction.

FB followed him at a distance along Rue Bonaparte and then along the river to the Quai de Conti. It did occur to him, as he observed the curly-black-haired student from behind, that he may have got the wrong person. Could love be playing a trick on him? He was self-aware enough to consider that his desperate need to reconnect with Mathilde could have affected his judgement. And yet he continued to put one foot in front of the other and carried on following the other man anyway.

Beyond the Rue des Beaux-Arts the young student had reached the Quai Malaquais and turned right. At the Place de L'Institut he stopped to cross the road and continued walking amongst the *bouquinistes* along the riverbank. It was as he stopped to look at some magazines at one of these stalls that FB caught a fresh view of the student's profile. He felt sure that the man holding up the copy of *Empédocle* was Mathilde's friend. But then again, had Mathilde's friend worn those black-framed spectacles? FB couldn't be sure.

He was like one of Maigret's young offsiders (though a rather indecisive one) as he followed the student fossicking along the riverbank stalls. When Gilles picked up a Frantz Fanon book and delved into his pocket for the francs to pay for it, FB felt that was confirmation enough to take the plunge. Hadn't Mathilde and her father been discussing Fanon at La Teste-de-Buch?

He hastened to the young man's side.

'Hello. *Vous êtes un ami de Mathilde Soubret?*'

The student looked surprised, perhaps too surprised to answer.

'*Moi aussi,*' FB went on. '*Mathilde a parlé de vous.* You are Gilles, no?'

This time the student nodded, but slowly, silently.

FB was overjoyed. *'Je la cherche,'* he said. And then in English: 'I am trying to get in touch with her.'

Now Gilles raised his eyebrows a little. 'You don't have her address, her telephone number?' he asked.

'Well, her address, yes, but not her number.'

'Do you study with her?'

'No, no.'

'Are you with the CGT? You don't look like you're with the FLN.'

FB sensed an undercurrent of hostility now. Did it have something to do with political allegiances?

'No, no,' he said, smiling. 'I have just recently been with her in Arcachon. With her family. I could not return with her to Paris because of my studies but now that I am here I would like to see her.'

Gilles frowned, perhaps sensing that the explanation given by FB wasn't quite true. He slipped the Fanon book and also the copy of *Empédocle* into his satchel. FB suspected that he was stealing the latter. Somehow Gilles gave the impression of thinking fast as he put the books away.

'Well,' he said, fastening his satchel strap, 'I don't have Mathilde's number with me. But I'd be happy to give it to you. We could meet later on. I have to go now.'

'Thank you,' FB said. 'I'd appreciate that.'

'Okay. Seven o'clock at the Brasserie les Arènes on Rue Linné. You know it?'

'Yes. Between Jussieu and the *Jardin.*'

'*Exactement.*'

'Okay then.'

'Yes. Okay.'

†

It seems true that FB's temperament, his interests, not to mention the sheer capacity of his mind had isolated him even in childhood, but now when I think of the air of solitude he always had about him in the bookshop and on those other occasions when I spoke with him, it is not that childhood isolation that I think about; it is simply the young FB standing under a blood-coloured awning across the road from 40 Rue Monge. It is also the young FB on the lonely trek from his lodgings in the fifth arrondissement to his classes with Professor Lacombe. And, finally, it is FB as he waits at an outdoor table at the Brasserie les Arènes on Rue Linné for Mathilde's friend to arrive and give him her number.

He admits in his diary that his hopes were high – so high, in fact, that he had convinced himself that Gilles might even arrange for Mathilde to come along to Rue Linné also. But seven o'clock went by without a sign of either of them, then seven thirty, then seven forty-five. From where he sat he could see the tall black and gold gates of the Jardin des Plantes and he began to feel as lonely as the small group of wallabies that lived in an enclosure there behind the gates.

He drank two coffees and two glasses of Bourgueil. At least the wallabies had each other. At 9 pm, when he paid his bill, the brasserie was full of students laughing and carousing but it might as well have been full of sand. Sand up to the ceiling. He felt as if he might choke from the utter aridity of his situation. He felt duped, terribly alone. He moved away from the brasserie, with sand spilling from his tweedy cuffs. He stepped out onto the street. He walked along to the gates of the gardens, knowing they'd be shut. As he looked in through the vertical columns between the bars the entire garden, its furry leaves, its humid stench, its republican canopy of tendrils and branches, seemed to tilt towards him. The whole of Paris now felt like a dark carnival. Lurid and fickle. Distraught, he turned and walked away.

Four

Four

17

Rhizome

IN THE WEEK AFTER FB DIED I DREAMT THAT ALL THE signs along the Great Ocean Road, the speed limit signs, the give way signs, the signs indicating the danger of land-slips and seasonal waterfalls, the no-camping, no-alcohol and no-sleeping-in-your-car signs, the Welcome to Lorne, Wye River, Apollo Bay etc. signs, and all the simple creek and place signs in between, including the signs warning motorists to watch out for crossing echidnas, koalas and kangaroos, were all painted black in honour of his memory. I think now of those funereal roadside blanks with an immense wistfulness due to their purely imaginary nature. How I wish I lived in a society that could honour its dead with such simple but momentous gestures. No words needed, no sculptures in totalitarian bronze, no sentimental caricatures, just a colour. A colour repeated. A colour to take away the hyperbole, to take away the caution and fear, the do's and dont's, the directions for how life should be lived and at what speed. All this replaced by a deeply quiet emotion.

In the end that is what it is about FB that has compelled me to linger for so long amongst his things: that deeply quiet emotion.

If you had spent decades chronicling the movement of sand, ostensibly in order to control that movement, you might in the end begin to wonder what it is about the human species that feels the need to organise nature so. Surely a desire to travel unimpeded in vehicles from A to B could not be the only justification for an obsessive alteration of organic forms? And yet the Victorian Country Roads Board would have it so. There, upon his return from France, FB Herschell sat, year after year, in the McKillop Street office, attempting to widen the parameters of the intellection of sand. He well understood the public purpose of his activities, but there was a private universe in them as well. And in that private universe was a city of his imagination, a city at night, where the tall elegant gates of the Jardin des Plantes slowly opened onto a humid darkness. A slow and stately music played in his mind as FB crept in amongst the shadows of the foliage to find the exiled wallabies on their little patch of manicured lawn. It is there that he dreamt himself laying down to sleep.

There, behind the barriers of the enclosure, behind the lined graphs and white charts, the ant-like statistics, the wind-vector diagrams and annotated directives, lies the scene: the quiet sadness of an Australian man, the tragic dignity of his inability to express it in any other way.

†

The initial obstacle FB encountered on his return was Gibbon's stubborn refusal to let him return to the part of the coast that had set him out on his course overseas in the first place. FB was told upon his return to work at the CRB office that the ongoing problem of Mr Lane's long beach road between Anglesea and the Split Point cliffs could wait, as could the situation at Eastern View. 'There's more pressing work out the back of Barwon Heads,' Gibbon declared. 'It'll certainly be the test of any expertise you've picked up from the French.'

So it was that FB began employing his knowledge along the ocean coast of the Bellarine Peninsula, which years before the returned World War I soldiers began their work had been the proposed starting point for the building of the Great Ocean Road. On Gibbon's suggestion, FB was helped by a group of Croatian women from the Nissen huts of East Geelong who, in floral headscarves and wide skirts, planted the marram grass so hard and well that the sand gathered around the grass with an efficiency that even FB couldn't quite believe. He'd come back from France with revolutionary lessons, with the examples of *les landes* and Cap Ferret still fresh in his mind, and they were having immediate results. The Gascony palisades he erected, combined

225

with the assiduity of the Croatian women's planting of the marram, saw the small area he first concentrated on – the sloping dune habitat along the Bluff Road just south-west of the mouth of the Barwon River – steadily changed.

Just as he had with Professor Lacombe on their trip to Arcachon and Cap Ferret, and during those strange and lonely weeks in Paris after their return, when his studies reached their crescendo in inverse proportion to the desolation of his heart, FB managed to mask his emotional turmoil in his dealings with Gibbon. In this way, his sadness came back to Australia as grumpiness, even arrogance. When Gibbon demanded an extended report on his studies in France, FB at first ignored him completely. Then, when Gibbon got shirty (as the saying went in those days), he consented to deliver a thirty-six-page report – but in French! Called in to Gibbon's high office to explain, FB's response was curt. When Gibbon pointed to the wad of staple-bound foolscap on the desk in front of him and demanded: 'What's the point of giving me this?', FB replied: 'You gave me no encouragement in these endeavours. In fact, you actively tried to block my path to Paris. But if I can go to the trouble of making the journey to the other end of the world, and of learning the language which holds the key to a lot of this research, then you can bloody well learn it too!' And with that FB got up and stormed out of the building.

He sat for the rest of the afternoon at the window of the front bar of the Corio Hotel in Yarra Street, nursing a single glass of stout and trying to calm himself down.

The problem Gibbon had was that, as far as his CRB bosses in Melbourne were concerned, Frank Herschell was a feather in his cap. There had been no-one amongst the engineers in the Melbourne office who'd shown the kind of initiative that Herschell had, and the news of his research trip, including the scholarship he attained to get him over there – which Gibbon had indeed tried to stymie out of pure one-upmanship – rubbed off on the whole of Gibbon's Geelong branch just as it had made its way up to the CRB hierarchy in Melbourne. It was indeed the case that in FB's absence, Gibbon and his cohort in McKillop Street had received an official commendation from the governor, which they all knew could be attributed to the official policy of fostering international relations. But Gibbon could no sooner have admitted that to FB than he could have read the report in French. Which meant of course that the defiance of FB initially refusing to submit his report, and then the wilfulness of him finally submitting it in a fashion unintelligible to Gibbon, could logically have been construed as the actions of a man who wanted to be dismissed from his post. At that stage however there was no way that Gibbon could have sacked him, not even for what his military cronies would have termed 'gross insubordination'. Unbeknowns to him FB's petulance in fact contained no risk at all, as Gibbon well knew he had to retain the jewel in his crown, even if it meant turning a blind eye to behaviour which enraged him.

It stands to reason, then, that any discussion of the actual technology of sand and its stabilisation was at that stage impossible between Gibbon and FB. And for the time being the work of the Croatian women continued apace with his encouragement out on Bluff Road and on the Thirteenth Beach road. As the introduced tussocks multiplied and grew, any inklings FB had of those hummocks becoming a living embodiment of the heaviness in his heart remained well out on the rim of his professional life. It seems fair though to suggest that he must nevertheless have begun to harbour such oblique correspondences between his anguish and his stabilisation methods from this time on – in the same secret way, perhaps, as he harboured the intuitions he found amongst Proust, Perec, Gracq, Mondrian and Albert Camus.

18

Subsidence

BEFORE FB LEFT PARIS, IT HAD BEEN IN RESPONSE TO HIS final submitted essay on Brémontier's work of the late 1700s that Professor Lacombe had finally showed his hand on the creation of the largest forest in Europe along the previously squelchy and unproductive magnificence of *les landes* on the Atlantic coast. Despite a fascination with the long-gone stilt-walking inhabitants of the marshes, and the fact that the Gascony coast was now a site of some personal loss and despair for him, FB sang the praises in the essay of Brémontier's grand project of planting out two hundred kilometres of coastal wetlands with the *Pinus pinaster* and the coastal dune with *gourbet*.

When he was summoned to Professor Lacombe's office after being awarded top marks he, understandably enough, presumed it was so that the professor could offer him his congratulations. But that was only part of the reason. By this stage, FB had been back from the Atlantic coast for many weeks. After the protests culminated in students setting fire to the Bourse, or Paris Stock Exchange, on 24 May, de Gaulle had been returned with a record-breaking majority in the elections of 23 and 30 June, and the dramatic events of May seemed almost as distant as Australia. On the very morning that FB was summoned to Lacombe's office he had risen at 5 am to go walking, after yet another restless night, and stood at the bar of the all-night *tabac* on Rue Gay-Lussac as the paving machinery of the municipality of the Île de France proceeded stealthily through the first light. These were the bitumen trucks come on de Gaulle's orders to seal the fate of history. For centuries the people of Paris had used the streets' cobblestones as their weapons against what they considered to be oppressive or unjust regimes. Only now did the machinery exist to remove the problem once and for all. FB, the *tabac* owner and one or two other early risers watched through freshly washed glass as the noisy machines began the process which would result in a thick black treacle of tar being layed over the pattern of the old stones.

A heavy silence inverted the *tabac* amid the noise of the dawn machines. FB was conscious of what he was looking at. This was quite literally the machinery of the state, everything the protests of May had been up against. The *tabac* owner and the two men cradling their coffees obviously felt the significance of what they were watching also. They did not need to ask for each other's

230

precise thoughts in the moment. No-one said a word.

Nor did Professor Lacombe when his tired-looking protégé entered his room. Lacombe gestured for FB to take a seat. Then the two sat in silence for what seemed to FB like a very long time.

Eventually Lacombe asked, 'Do you ever wonder how the shepherds would have felt?'

FB's mind was weary, his whole being exhausted. He thought he must have missed something.

'When they drained *les landes*,' Lacombe explained. 'When they transformed their homes, their sheep pastures, their way of life.'

It was phrased as a question but FB was feeling too slow. Though something was beginning to dawn.

'Do you know in 1948 there was a forest fire in *les landes* that killed fifty-two people?'

'No,' said the bewildered student. 'I didn't know that.'

'Your assignment was well researched, well executed, as is evidenced by your results.'

Silence.

'Thank you,' FB managed finally.

Lacombe dismissed this with a wave of his hand.

'But I wonder what the consequences will ultimately be if we drain every similar landscape of its moisture in the name of commercial productivity.'

FB frowned.

'A world without stilts, perhaps,' Lacombe said with a smile.

FB managed a weak smile too.

And then, quite unexpectedly, the professor asked: 'How is Mathilde?'

FB was shocked. Of the three questions he'd been asked so far this was easily the hardest to answer.

'I don't know,' he said.

Professor Lacombe nodded. 'I thought as much.'

'I haven't seen her since our time in Arcachon,' FB admitted.

'Yes. Well, yesterday I received this envelope, enclosed in a letter addressed to me. She did not know your address?'

FB looked confused.

'Well, whatever the case, I have been asked to hand this on to you.'

Lacombe passed the small white envelope across the desk. It was addressed simply to 'Francis Herschell'. Turning it over FB saw that on the back there was an address in Munich.

'It seems from her letter to me that she has joined a student delegation to discuss the situation internationally. Prague, Vietnam, Greece, Chicago. But I'm sure she will let you know all that.'

'Thank you,' FB said again in a quiet voice.

'It is no trouble.'

The professor stood up then, signalling the end of the meeting. 'So, you will return home now that your studies here are over?'

'Yes,' FB replied, also getting up.

Lacombe walked his student to the door. 'And of course we will stay in touch, Francis.'

'Yes, of course. Thank you, Professor.'

The two men shook hands and the Australian scholarship student left through the door.

†

FB's papers do not include the exact contents of the letter Mathilde sent from Munich, but they do hint at some of its ingredients. It seems certain enough that she mentioned Herbert Marcuse, Mario Savio, Bobby Kennedy, Alexander Dubček, Rudi Dutschke. She also alluded to her possible involvement in the events of 24 May, when the Bourse was set on fire. Whether or not the letter became any more personal than that is unclear, although given the fact that FB would make cryptic allusions to it in his private papers for many years to come it seems that it might have. If nothing else, it's clear that Mathilde felt the need to demonstrate to FB that leaving La Teste-de-Buch to return to the fray was not a decision she took lightly, and would not be a decision she would recoil from, or waste.

The morning after his final meeting with Lacombe, FB was back at the all-night *tabac* on Rue Gay-Lussac, having been sleepless once again as he digested the letter's contents. Once again the paving crew were there, tamping down the concrete over which they would smear the top layer of oily black asphalt. An acrid smell was in the air, struggling for control over the scent of cigarettes, coffee and almonds. FB sat in the window, alone at one of only three tables, watching the method of the paving crews, their discussions, the angles of their Gitanes, the smears on their overalls, the cohesion of the machinery which nevertheless clanked and roared primitively in the birdless dawn.

She also seems to have mentioned Mexico in the letter; the possibility that she might go there for a meeting potentially more effective and purposeful than the one she was attending in Munich. It seems as if she was letting FB know that she did not underestimate the price he had paid. That she would not waste his pain. He records having flinched at 3 am in his room, and then that he sat bolt upright in the dark, panting, as it occurred to him that somehow he was being martyred for the cause. Was he supposed to be proud of her engagement, proud that somehow his suffering had made its own contribution to the flames licking the Bourse, to the creation of a new world? Momentarily the letter not only saddened him, but panicked and disgusted him. By 4 am he was dressed and out on the puce-coloured streets again.

As he sat looking out the window of the *tabac*, it was obvious the machinery of the state was still very much in control, despite what she might think. Already the regulars at the bar were growing used to the sound of the machines, resigned to the idea. Was this what it was like when the Nazi tanks rolled into the boulevards in 1940? he wondered. Was it just a matter of acclimatisation? Millions on the streets one minute, silent coffees and Armagnacs the next. Let's just talk football, shall we? Or about the Jew who lives on the corner. Take our ticket in the Loterie Nationale, talk taxes, food prices, blind ourselves with particulars to avoid staring into the bigger picture, the deeper river. In her courtesy, she had written to inform him, if only by implication, that he was back there in the ruck, and that she was a topmost apple on the tree. Was she thanking him for that? He suspected so.

With the new light the day began to warm up, but FB sat frozen in his seat in the *tabac*, amidst the grinding, screaming apparatus of the road gang. Perhaps Gilles had let her know how desperate he was? Was that what had made her write?

Two nuns walked past on the other side of the window, one with a soccer ball in her arms, the other with a green ukulele. They stopped briefly as one pointed out the paving crew to the other. They began to discuss what was going on, the covering over of the cobblestones. Then suddenly the ball spilt from the nun's arms and rolled out onto the half-constructed tarmac. FB watched as a lightly built man in his twenties deftly flicked the ball up to himself, wiped it against his blue overalls and returned it to the nun. They had a brief exchange, at the end of which the young worker shrugged his shoulders and raised his hands, as if to absolve himself of any responsibility. The nuns frowned at him, and continued on into the morning.

It was another layer being installed between nature and culture. The cobbles were made by hand, and they fitted in the hand. Mathilde had hurled them herself, on this very street, on the night of the barricades. But now she was away at a meeting in Munich. And then she would be off to another one in Mexico. FB drained his cup. The future, it seemed, was sealed.

†

On the flight home, perhaps because he was in mid-air, beholden to no ground, hardly even to gravity, he found himself feeling differently. The May demonstrations had ultimately achieved a thirty-five percent wage rise, and he was obviously still in her thoughts. Could the plane do a U-turn, he wondered, right there above the Aegean Sea? He would wait for her, in Paris, under the florist's awning opposite 40 Rue Monge, with his integrity intact. He would propose a new beginning for them both in Australia, where more than half the roads had not even been cobbled yet, let alone sealed in hot asphalt. There was an openness there, he would tell her, the sand was free to blow itself about, there was not such a stubborn edifice to remove. Things were moving, progressing, blooming even. A bird had room to fly.

He checked himself. Who was he kidding? The jumbo jet was hurtling south and would not be turning back. And here was the hostess, with the cold beer he'd ordered, as if to confirm that this was so.

19

Backshore

FB HAD DEVELOPED A REPUTATION AS BOTH A GENTLEMAN and a bit of a clown amongst the Croatian women he had recruited to plant the marram grass out on Bluff Road. This was largely because he was comfortable in their company. At home on Milipi Avenue with his mother, however, his mind was full of murderous thoughts and other dark flights of the imagination. His mother was glad to have him home again, but he cast her as an overweight pigeon who, once stuck in the depth of the backyard birdbath, would not be able to extricate herself. He imagined her feathers growing dark and heavy until she became leaden in the water. And there she drowned. His mother-pigeon. But that was not all. Upon finding her dead he proceeded to wring her neck and cooked her just as Elizabeth David recommended in her book *French Provincial Cooking.*

It was in this kind of volatile atmosphere that books became more of a saviour than ever. He read *The Lucky Country* by Donald Horne in those first months of his return and copied the following quote into his journal: *'Australia is a lucky country run mainly by second rate people who share its luck.'* Such, he felt, was his life at the CRB, where Gibbon and he ground against each other like tectonic plates, thereby causing any amount of shudders and shockwaves in the department. Amid all this the Croatian women were a fond relief. He got on well with them, enjoying their directness, their practical intelligence and unassuming air. Because of his time in France he felt his horizons had widened, and the women certainly allowed for that worldliness, given their non-Australian origins. A couple of them had visited France themselves before migrating to Victoria, and so it was the case that he could find himself fixing up string-lines for the palisades beside Bluff Road while discussing the merits of the SNCF with a bent-over mother of four called Maria, or the steeping methods required for the cooking of snails with a compassionate beauty called Vera Kaloper. He would share jokes with the women, too, sometimes even at the expense of the French, but generally the butt of their humour had more in common with the wryness of Donald Horne than the seriously slippery slopes of Vichy. The women enjoyed FB's capacity for irreverence and grew fond enough of him to rib him from time to time about little personal things, like the forever bobbling pom-poms on his outlandish tam-o'-shanter, or even bigger things like the fact that he still remained unmarried.

These were his handsome years, after all, there seems little doubt of that. Recently returned from Europe, he carried himself with confidence and sophistication in public and dressed with a more subtle flair than he had before he'd left Geelong. Internally, of course, he felt anything but dapper but this deeper discrepancy would lessen while he worked with the women on the dunes. Around Gibbon, however, as is evidenced by his stunt of submitting the report in French, he quite often allowed the tension to come to the fore.

The task out at Barwon Heads was nothing on the scale of what Brémontier had done by planting the pines of *les landes*, but as the marram grass so successfully took over the dunes just south of the Barwon River mouth, and as his graphs and measurements altered accordingly, something about the process began to unnerve him. It is hard to tell whether his eventual change of mind on the planting of marram grass had as much to do with upsetting his superior as it did with his newly awakened *longue durée* view of history. Or whether indeed – and this truly is perhaps the key enigma at the heart of his quiet life – it came about as a product of first his flourishing with, then his rejection by, Mathilde.

Whatever the case, by the beginning of 1970, with him still barred by Gibbon from reassessing the problems out

beyond Anglesea, and with the majority of his work therefore still dealing with the issues of drift on Bluff Road (he
also worked during this period on proposed traffic lights
in Grovedale, an analysis of a bluestone bridge at Waurn
Ponds, and the pros and cons of a general philosophical
shift in the department towards roundabouts), both his
reading and ordering of books and his actual work on
the dunes began to seriously dovetail. What he had seen
around the Bassin d'Arcachon, and what he had learnt
of his own heart in the mill behind the salt pastures of
La Teste-de-Buch, had combined to set him out on what
would become his own quietly revolutionary path.

†

Long before he breathed a word of what he had in mind,
he dreamt one night in his single bed in Milipi Avenue
of sand lying on top of a road, like salt spilt from a
shaker, with a group of hooded plovers sitting at a table
nearby with a red-and-white checked tablecloth, clinking
glasses, toasting the arrangement with champagne. He
woke up amused and recorded this dream in his journal.
The following day he wrote also of a spotless black road
running through a landscape of steep hummocks, with a
sign beside the road reading:

IN MOURNING. DRIVE SLOWLY.
WORLD'S LONGEST CONTINUOUS GRAVE.

He writes that in the far distance of this dream he could see '*M walking on a hill-line. Know that I will only stop weeping once she has gone over the horizon.*'

But where exactly was that horizon, and how far into the future could his naked eyes possibly see?

†

One has to consider how deeply changed FB must have been by his experience in France to think about turning on its head not only what he had been trained to believe in Australia but what had been confirmed for him over there as well. Yet perhaps one should also consider that these were quasi-revolutionary times, even in Australia. When he listened to reports on the wireless of the Vietnam moratorium marches Dr Jim Cairns was leading in Melbourne and saw pictures in the *Herald* of the thousands walking through the streets, was he tempted to get involved? It seems not. There is no hint of sentiment at the idea of thousands of people wresting control from dark uniforms on their city streets. Nor is there any indication in his papers of his actual political position at that point or at any point afterwards. But as the planting of the marram grass by the Croatian women grew ridiculously successful – *Ammophila arenaria Ammophila arenaria Ammophila arenaria* – it seems he had begun to walk off on his own along the beach from time to time and stand away at a distance, a lonely figure of the striated air, looking back on the dunes growing ever taller amid the teal streaks and charcoal flecks of the stormy Bass Strait. What I presume he was thinking out there on his own on the beach, amid his ongoing calculation of the proliferation of new gradients, was whether he could refine the experience he'd gained. Could he de-acclimatise? Could three long centuries of engineering progress be allowed to drift?

He was beginning to wonder.

†

I would not be honest if I did not admit to wondering myself whether or not I should presume to know what FB was thinking there on the beach all those years ago. Can I presume? Perhaps, given that there are such strong indicators there in his archive. Nevertheless, I ask myself two separate but interconnected questions. One, whether the FB I have created, or re-created, in these pages bears any real resemblance to the man who actually lived. And two, whether the written word is enough: pages of white sand full of black insects wriggling and darting about, each diary entry and journal note like the thrip-infested coast after a significant spike in temperature. Perhaps, like the thrips' proliferation in heat, FB's emotions hatched when he wrote – but what about the cooler periods in between? The time when he wasn't writing? I've come to think that a man who is, on the one hand, capable of writing down his dream of nestling with the wallabies of the Jardin des Plantes, and on the other, the precise calculations of the length, formation, pavement and seal of numerous sections of a coast road, has a range so broad that he is destined for personal difficulties. In any case, that range does not leave much outside the realms of possibility imagined by an interested observer.

Nor do these words, which he wrote in March 1971: *'Everything suddenly too steep, the desire to make things permanent, to stabilise, has my emotions at 1:3.'*

Or on 6 June the same year: *'M in my heart as either lover or artefact. How to unmake her in the landscape. Is this fit work? Is engineer the right verb?'*

†

The law of gradients when it comes to marram grass is a factor that can be used on both sides of the argument. On the one hand, as the good folk of Port Fairy discovered so long ago, the matting rhizomes of the plant combined with its lack of thirst, its salt tolerance and compatibility with the tiny meiofaunal communities that thrive in sand, sees it quickly trap the sand around itself, taking the pressure of drift-granules away from ad hoc colonial streets until the dune steepens, the grass grows tall in its tufts, and a genuine hummock almost completely free of slacks and blowouts is developed. (The dune bailiffs of the Jutland coast, whose Ammophila arenaria *is a native species, had figured this out way back when there were still only wild horses inhabiting Cap Ferret.) On the other hand, marram grass,*

245

in all its assiduous colonising eagerness, can also be viewed as the floral rabbit of the Australasian coastline, to which it is not native. When introduced it quickly proliferates, hence it being, like the rabbit and the blackberry, a darling of the early Acclimatisation Society of Victoria. By significantly altering the scale and contour of foredunes, marram grass dominated the native plant community, also disadvantaging native shorebirds which rely for nesting and general habitat on the continuing mobility and circulation of sand. The stabilisation for which the marram grass is so effective alters the porous interplay between sea and shore, preventing sand from continuing its amphibious cyclical motion, thus creating steep dune gradients which then become vulnerable to tidal erosion.

The general thrust of this summary of the marram grass debate could easily be found these days on any number of websites, in a little under five minutes. But these private paragraphs, written on the pale green CRB notepaper that itself seems to proliferate amongst the hummock of FB's archive almost as vigorously as the plant in question, were composed on 6 December 1971. The Acclimatisation Society of Victoria, which FB mentions, was by then long defunct in its original form, but rest assured its philosophies very much endured, particularly in the field of flora. Which makes FB's subversion of the law of gradients here, by including the counterargument against marram grass and thereby putting the very stabilisation work that he had long been passionate about at risk, quite remarkable.

As is his scrawled inclusion of the following quote from the end of *À la recherche du temps perdu* at the bottom of the very same pale green page:

Authentic art has no use for proclamations . . . it accomplishes its work in silence.

20

Drift Line

I N THINKING ABOUT FB'S EXPERIENCES IN FRANCE I
continually wonder how it must have been for all the
thousands of ordinary people: the workers at the Renault
factory on the Île Seguin, at Sud Aviation in Nantes, the
families and friends of the two hundred drowned in the
Seine near the Pont Saint-Michel, the families and friends
of those boys sent off to battle in Vietnam. Even the guys
holding the riot shields on the night of the barricades, the
living police in their protective uniforms, even they must
have felt small, invisible, trodden upon. But it's what you
do with that smallness, that invisibility, that counts. For a
brief moment in May '68, a large part of what Professor
Lacombe might have described as the meiofaunal population of France stood up, staked a claim, shouted to be
heard, only to find themselves described by de Gaulle as
chienlit, or *chie-en-lit*: 'shit in bed'.

In actual fact, the French students and workers were perhaps worse off than meiofauna, which, although microscopically tiny and seemingly insignificant, are perfectly happy in their sand-bound situation. So happy, indeed, that, as far as any biologist, entomologist or dune morphologist can ascertain, they have absolutely no need for the concept of 'happiness' at all.

Extended metaphors like this, which often seem a tad facile, can nevertheless be useful. FB certainly thought so. A former colleague of his at the CRB, whom I was introduced to after FB's death, could barely wipe the smile off his face as he explained to me how back in the seventies FB co-opted the British pejorative term 'rotter' – as in 'you rotter!' – to create an in-house nickname for Gibbon amongst select CRB and volunteer crew. The esteemed regional manager was thus known in certain circles as 'the Rotifer', which turns out to be a phylum of meiofauna quite prolific in the local dunescapes of southern Victoria, and which quite obviously could be employed to refer to

Gibbon in either its full or rather more slangy and shortened version. The colleague of FB's told me this story over
a drink in the Sawyers Arms Tavern. He was keen for me
to understand how funny FB could be and thus how much
he was liked by the rank and file. When we'd finished our
drinks and were saying goodbye out on the street, he said
wistfully, 'By the end he appeared around the place as a
quiet and old-fashioned gentleman, what with the vintage
French car and the tweeds and the like. But he was as
vibrantly alive and progressive as you could ever imagine.'

*Rotifers, nematodes, mystacocarids, tardigrades, gastrotrichs, turbel-
larians, kinorhynchs.*

I came upon this short list amongst FB's papers a few
weeks after being told of the nickname he'd coined for
Gibbon. It made me laugh, of course, and also got me
wondering what use he could potentially have made of
the other names. It is just a little list and could easily
be overlooked by those with less interest in the private
dimensions of such a man. For myself it only added to the
strange desire that's been with me ever since he died: the
desire to have known him better.

†

It was during the years when he was sequestered by
Gibbon into the stabilisation work at Barwon Heads that

FB first met my neighbour Anna Nielson. At the time, she was living amongst the community of Croatian migrants of East Geelong. On her evening walks along the Barwon River, Anna had got to know a number of the women who were planting the grasses with FB out near Barwon Heads. She would talk to the women about their children, also their gardens, the vegetable patches and grapevines which had begun to thrive in the southern river loam amongst the light industry of the streeted riverbank. Often she would end up being coaxed through the dusk into one or another of their houses and showered with food and homemade wine. It was during one of these house visits that she heard about the grasses they were planting for the CRB man on the dunes out on the coast near the mouth of the river. She showed an interest and, encouraged by her neighbours, agreed to go out with them on the Queen's Birthday holiday to lend a hand.

In the end, she only worked with them for one day. The hours were long and the work was backbreaking. An older Croatian man named Lex Ravlich had arrived at Anna's door in a brown Commer van at 6 am sharp. Lex Ravlich acted as an agent for the larger market gardeners out on the flat alluvial fields on the volcanic plain between Geelong and Melbourne. When harvest time came, or onion grass needed to be slashed, he would, for a fee, round up the women of his community, few of whom had cars of their own at this stage, and transport them out to those fields near Lara, Little River and the You Yangs to earn some money. When the work was due to begin on the dunes of Bluff Road, Gibbon had suggested to FB that he contact Lex Ravlich and arrange for the women to plant the marram grass during breaks in their market garden schedule. So in the grey dawn Anna Nielson joined eight other women in Lex Ravlich's Commer, and they travelled out through the salt pastures and marshy guzzles of Moolap towards the dunes.

FB was there to meet them at the designated spot, and he and Anna were briefly introduced, after which she joined the Croatian women in traipsing back along the dunes to where they had left off the previous day. Anna had always found the women so warm and friendly but now, after showing her the planting method and the area to be covered, they hardly said another word until the first break – a quick fifteen-minute snack at 10 am. By that stage Anna's back was aching, her face was red with a mixture of exertion and windburn, and the prospect of having to go to the toilet by squatting in the nearest dune slack was not that appealing.

By lunchtime she had stinging scratches on her hands, and her knees were so sore it made her aching back seem bearable. The group sat to eat in the lee of she-oaks one hundred yards back towards the golf course boundary. FB joined them, having worked elsewhere all morning directing two local blokes who were erecting the palisades (or 'slat fences' as he was calling them locally) in the foredunes on the ocean side of the plantings. He noticed immediately that the new friend of the Croatian women was quite flushed and exhausted. He could also see that she was not complaining or drawing attention to herself. She was even managing to laugh along with some of the jokes the women were making at Lex Ravlich's expense.

FB made his way over to Anna Nielson to thank her for coming along. As she explained to me later on after his death, she found him courteous and amusing, and could see that the other women felt the same. She laughed loudly when she told me: 'We were a bit like his little harem in the dunes. It was positively *Bedouin!*'

Anna no doubt discovered over the years ahead just how far from such a mindset FB was on that Queen's Birthday holiday in the middle of 1971. If there was to be a romance in the dunes for him, it could only be at the other end of the world.

†

I like to think that to a casual acquaintance of FB's in Geelong at that time, the somewhat distant charm he exhibited to the Croatian women, and to Anna Nielson on that Queen's Birthday in 1971, could easily have appeared as entirely consistent with the reticent tone of his public personality before he went to France. However, whereas the interior remove of his persona before France had more to do perhaps with the doting of his mother, and therefore with general feelings of constriction and guilt, the social distance he displayed after his return actually had a different quality, an undertow perhaps resembling that which I found so compelling and mysterious when I first read his book on the Great Ocean Road.

On page 64, of *The Great Ocean Road: Dune Stabilisation and Other Engineering Difficulties*, he had this to say:

> *In case of instability, or even dramatic subsidence, on such a public carriageway, it is not altogether spurious to ask the question of what, at heart, has caused the incident: the road or the dune? Inevitably, the engineer will cast the faultiness of the road (and perhaps even of the road-maker involved) as the culprit, but the dune morphologist would view it from the other perspective. He would point to the nature of the dune, to its inclinations, even to its personality, in order to demonstrate how the situation came to arise. Perhaps the nub of the problem, however, lies not in one thing or another, but in the relationship between the two.*

It is possible that the kangaroo disappearing down the hole on Mr Lane's private road between Anglesea and Sunnymeade may have inspired this reflection of FB's. But what struck me when I first read his book during the research for my own work on the road was the mention, in such an apparently dry and minor local publication in 1982, of a sand dune having a *personality*. This was highly unusual, to put it mildly. There seemed to be a consciousness below the surface of a concept like that which was almost audible in the sea air around me. If, as far as this civil engineer FB Herschell was concerned, sand dunes had personalities, then the whole ocean environment into which the famous road was set could have a character, a voice even, which could speak, in the wind, even *sing*.

†

Slowly, slowly he carried on with his life during this period and slowly, slowly his mindset changed. He rejoined the Moorabool Chamber Orchestra for a time but soon seemed to grow tired of it. From time to time he drank at the pub with colleagues, he travelled on the train to Melbourne to visit his favourite libraries and bookshops and to attend classes at the Alliance Française. Then, nearly five years after his return from France, in a note on March 1973 (once again on the faded, grass-green CRB paper), he wrote: '*Have begun to see the marram grass as barricades. But would they unplant for me?*'

Marram grass barricades. Instead of the diverse ready-made barricades of the Latin Quarter, where he had seen anything and everything scrounged and piled up high in order to resist the aggression of the state, now suddenly he sees laid out before him, in so many serried ranks, barricades consisting of one, and only one, species. These barricades have not swelled up out of the place itself but have been inserted into the scene to stem the rioting effects of wind on sand. And it is he who has inserted them.

The local authority that had been invested in him due to his studies in Paris, his field trips to Arcachon and his surveying of the theories of everyone from Brémontier to Bagnold, had not prepared him for this. Rather, it was something else that had prepared him: an entirely invisible deepening that came with the consideration of his plight from all the various angles. He had not been rejected for another man, this much was clear. Instead, he had been left behind for an *idea*, an idea of a society so much better than what the aftermath of World War II had created. His heart's wrench, his anger and jealousy not towards another man but towards a *cause*, was gradually transforming into a kind of emulation. In short, he began to pay attention. He was no longer distracted. If nothing else, Mathilde had taught him – not Lacombe, not Gibbon – how the environment of the dunes could become more than just the object of his intellect, the sand archive more than just a furrow for his love.

After six years, the stabilisation methods used from Bluff Road at Barwon Heads and along Thirteenth Beach seemed themselves to have justified what some of Gibbon's cohort in the CRB liked to call his 'junket to Froggyland'. No longer was there sand spilling out over the tarmac that ran along the ballowed hills and hummocks. The marram grass and the palisades had steepened and contoured the hummocks to such an extent that a farmer called Abrahams, whose property backed onto the golf club from the nor'west, had begun to complain about the blocking of sightlines from his farmhouse. Never mind the improvement of his pastures, now he was concerned about his ocean view. At first FB was tempted to use Abrahams' protest as a catalyst for the counterargument he was considering putting to Gibbon. 'Perhaps,' he could say, 'we should consider ameliorating the situation somewhat.' But no, in the end he decided, good Catholic boy that he was, that that would be in bad faith. And after all, the stats told the story. His 'Incidence of Sand Drifts on Road' graph clearly showed how he had achieved Gibbon's ends. The lessening of the frequency and size of the black ink bars denoting sand drift on the graph is marked from 1969 onwards. All that sand, spilt from the shaker, was now retained amongst FB's slats and rhizomes – and no amount of aesthetic complaints would ever convince old Gibbon that that wasn't a damn fine thing.

So instead FB settled on the only course available to

him. He took the philosophical course of the utmost sincerity, and it is that course, along with his romantic heart, that I felt rolling in so powerfully beneath the prose of his slim little book.

21

South of Brémontier

ALWYN GIBBON WAS GETTING ON IN AGE, THERE WAS NO doubt about that. But with that ageing came his 'vast experience of managing the transport needs of the state'. And never before, in all his long years in the office in McKillop Street, had he heard anything like it.

> *A magnificent life is waiting just around the corner, and far, far away. It is waiting like the cake is waiting when there's butter, milk, flour and sugar. This is the realm of freedom. It is an empty realm. Here man's magnificent power over nature has left him alone with himself, powerless. It is the boredom of youth without a future.*
>
> Henri Lefebvre

FB had waited until a mood of confidence was upon him. He needed the full force of his ego to withstand the scorn he knew his superior would pour upon his idea. In his head, in his bedroom, with his mother snoring loudly on the other side of the wall, he had rehearsed it countless times. 'This is no longer the Enlightenment,' he would say. 'Such Grand Projects are now seen for what they are: violent impositions on our natural inheritance by a wilfully ignorant human society.'

But no, he wouldn't get far with language like that. Nor would he succeed by citing the example of *les landes*, how no land in the 1970s could be viewed as it was back in Brémontier's time: as a nothing space, terra nullius, a wasteland. 'Do you ever wonder how the shepherds would have felt? When they drained *les landes*. When they transformed their homes, their sheep pastures, their way of life.' Even the words of the esteemed Professor Lacombe of the University of Paris would have no effect, for, at the bottom of things, Gibbon and his friends despised academics.

So he decided to keep the 'fancy stuff' out of it. He would simply suggest that, on closer examination of the particulars of the local scene, and from what he had observed of the circumstances in France, he had come to think that marram grass — *Ammophila arenaria Ammophila arenaria etc.* — was in fact the solution of another epoch and that in the Australian twentieth century it should logically be viewed as too invasive a species to justify its undoubted capacity to stabilise the dune landscape.

He knew that Gibbon would scoff at this, too; that FB would be written off as a Whitlam man, virtually

a communist in a department which had always bene-
fited from a more traditional, not to say conservative,
approach. But there was nothing FB could do about
that, no way he could paint the picture of what he had
seen in France, what he had painted on the walls of
Paris with his own hand, nor how he had finally understood the potential violence of excessive infrastructure
when he saw the cobblestones of the Latin Quarter
asphalted over.

It was a Friday morning in June 1974 when he
eventually knocked on the door of Gibbon's office.
The road signs of the entire country were about to be
switched from imperial to metric and FB was hoping that
Gibbon would be distracted by the details of that move,
the deadline for which was looming at the end of the
month. He had the names of the array of native plants
that would replace the marram grass at hand. He had the
recommendations of two government botanists and also
the transcript of Baron von Mueller's original advice to
the pioneer settlers of Port Fairy, which of course they
had rejected in favour of the quicker and easier solution
the baron had subsequently furnished them with. He
didn't expect Gibbon to be swayed by such evidence, but
he had it anyway. In his head, as well as in his briefcase.
The rejection of the native solution by Port Fairy was a
turning point for the colony and this would be another
one. He had a flow chart demonstrating how the phasing
out of *Ammophila arenaria* could be achieved without a

detrimental effect on the sand drift on the road. It was only a question of time. It would be a decade-long project. He had the support of local volunteer groups who would assist with the labour. And then there were the Croatian women, whose reliability was proven.

As he began to speak, in the hard-backed chair opposite Gibbon's desk, his heart began to sink. It was a bright winter's day, the sea glare everywhere in the streets. Strong Corio light poured through the window behind Gibbon's head along with the sound of the locally made cars driving below.

Immediately FB could hear how outlandish the idea sounded, how impractical, how *contrary*. It could not be *engineered*. He had begun with full guns blazing but was soon running out of ammunition. He attempted to outline the debate for Gibbon's benefit, but all his superior wanted to know was: 'What has this got to do with the roads?'

'Well, the roads are borne by the landscape, Alwyn. The right management of the landscape is critical to the perpetuity of the roads.'

'Correct me if I'm wrong,' Gibbon interrupted, 'but this is not a question of erosion is it?'

'Well, yes, it is, on the seaward side.'

Gibbon sniggered. 'Yes, well, when was the last time we had to manage a road on the *seaward* side of sand dunes? They call that the beach. Are you out of your mind, Frank?'

Perhaps for a moment, behind the insouciant and precocious exterior he was in the habit of adopting with Gibbon, his confidence crumbled. He wanted to unpick the seam, to pull out all the grass he had stitched into the sand. He wanted to cut down the entire forest of *les landes*, to see the stilt-walkers squelching again across the marshes, to allow Cap Ferret to shift about in the currents. In just the flicker of an eye he digested the *belatedness*, and therefore the *impossibility*, of the task. And he knew that Gibbon had noticed that flicker of doubt. From there he wasn't sure where on earth he could run.

He composed himself. He lived in a provincial town, made of butter, milk, flour and sugar, at the ends of the earth. Of course such a vision would seem impossible.

'Is this not the exact opposite approach to that you have been recommending ever since you returned from F-F-France?' Gibbon spat the word out like an expletive.

'No, these views are canvassed in my report on my findings in France. If you'd read it, you'd know that.'

Gibbon's face flushed, then went pale, like a bushfire had passed over it. He shook his head slowly from side to side and glared at FB. 'Your report's bloody well written in French!' he shouted.

The regional manager's shout took a long time to subside in the room. For a few moments the two men sat listening to its slow decay.

'Well, anyway,' FB said eventually, with a dismissive wave of his hand, 'I demand the right to evolve.'

22

Granulation

I T TOOK ALWYN GIBBON SEVERAL MONTHS — EIGHT, IN
fact — to relieve Frank Herschell of his duties with
sand. By March 1975 FB was writing to Professor
Lacombe in Paris about his fears of his dismissal. *'To be
removed from the dunes would be a significant intellectual loss to
me,'* he wrote. *'Especially given that the revolution I now know
you were always alluding to during my time in France has finally
occurred in my thinking.'*

Whether or not FB actually believed that Gibbon
would have the conviction to follow through with the
threat is unclear, but by the beginning of April he was left
in no doubt. Whatever Gibbon's other qualities, he was
certainly determined and, as they say, once he had made
his mind up about something there was no stopping him.

As it turned out, his most powerful weapon in his
transferring of FB's duties was the controversial report

written in French. Knowing full well that FB was, due to his international experience, viewed as a golden child at the CRB head office, Gibbon decided he should be hoist on his own petard. FB's original report seems sadly now to have been lost, but sitting in the CRB state archives in Melbourne, which are now housed under the VicRoads umbrella, is the complete English translation of the report which Gibbon commissioned from a French translator, a Mrs Frida Appleby, in August of 1974.

It is because of that report, which extols the enterprise and virtue of the planting of *Ammophila arenaria* along the French Atlantic coast, that he was able to convince his head office in Melbourne that the efficacy of Frank Herschell's work on sand dune stabilisation had run its course. For how, as Gibbon argued, could a CRB employee be sent at great expense to Paris, France, in order to learn from historically proven methods so as to employ those methods successfully in the local field, only to recommend the diametrically opposite approach only a few years after his return? Was he suffering from amnesia, or a rebellious form of parochialism? Could he not read his own French?

Of course, quite apart from the fact that the trip to France was not at the CRB's expense but achieved largely through a scholarship FB had himself proactively attained, his report is indeed very convincing. But FB's borrowing of Camus' line demanding the 'right to evolve' in that crucial meeting with Gibbon in June 1974 is at the heart of the issue. The seeds of his own revolutionary thinking are, as he said to Gibbon in that meeting, to be found in the report, if one reads it closely. Not once but twice he refers to emerging evidence pointing to the critical significance of maintaining marshlands in a littoral environment – which casts the draining and foresting of the enormous area of *les landes* in a questionable light. And with respect to marram grass – or *gourbet*, as it is referred to in the report – he does speculate about some of the problems that might arise due to its extremely hardy qualities of proliferation.

But it has to be said that these are only seeds of what he later came to think. For the most part, FB's report contained everything that Gibbon must have been looking for, even going so far as to suggest the possible planting of pine forests to convert Australian marshlands into productive forestry environments. This kind of talk was so far removed from what FB was now proposing – the exploration of the potential of a mixture of palisades and a more diverse native planting in order to stabilise the sand without destroying the historical features of the landscape and habitat – that Gibbon's suggestion that Frank Herschell was in need of new challenges within the department seemed plausible enough.

What was at stake here, though, was the plausibility of FB's deep philosophical shift. And in the years ahead he came to realise how unsuccessful he had been in communicating that change of position. But how,

I wonder, *could* he have communicated it, how could he really, being the man he was? Was he to tell his former champions in the Melbourne head office about the bird-cage door Mathilde had opened in the *tabac* at Clamart? Was he to regale them with the conversations he heard over a disconnected black telephone sitting on a tree stump in Saint-Sulpice? Was he to describe what it felt like to step outside a river of people flowing through the streets of their city chanting '*Sartre, au musée! Sartre, au musée!*'? Or should he describe to them the confusion, the painful mystification he felt when he realised that there existed in the world a beautiful young woman for whom love could be best expressed through an ideal of social justice? And how he had been abandoned to that, left alone in an old circular mill in a remnant patch of the saltmarsh he was now mourning the loss of?

For years it nagged at him: this failure to communicate. The way the disciplines of the heart and mind, the public and the private, divide us. He realised how hamstrung he was by his own *endemic* reticence, propagated as it probably was by being cuffed off a stool as a child for imagining a whole world in the ingredients of a cake bowl. With a mediocre adversary like Gibbon he was full of pluck, but in the general run of life it all remained underneath. As it did for the most part in the pages of his book.

But still, I noticed something.

†

He was assigned freeway ramps, kerbing and channel-ling, roundabouts, and grew especially fond of bridges. Ironically, his financial situation was improved by him being transferred off the dunes and was even further improved when his mother passed away. Intriguingly, he gives this only a cursory mention in his diary, writing with a complete lack of sentiment about clearing out his parents' belongings and staying on in the house, to which he made no alterations.

Gradually, without his mother's rule, the house, rather than just his single bedroom, began to fill up with books. In late 1976, with his extra funds, he imported the 1962 metallic blue Renault Ondine from France. It was exactly the same model as that in which Pierre Green had driven Lacombe and he around Cap Ferret.

I have not yet discovered the paperwork covering the importing of the Ondine amongst his papers but I keep finding the indent order forms and invoices for books and marvel at the extent of his interests. Right through the years after his exile from the dunes he continued to order widely: everything from books of Portuguese poetry from City Lights in San Francisco, to monographs on Japanese aqueducts from Kelly & Walsh in Hong Kong. He bought the latest American fiction from Strand Bookstore in New York, and European psychoanalytic theory and Estonian liturgical music from Charing Cross in London. He made extensive notes about the Frankfurt School, but also about Telford and Brunel, and Scottish Enlightenment painters.

Yet all the overseas orders, the reading and the taking of notes are of course no inoculation against perceptions of sadness. On the contrary. A single man shut away with his intellectual obsessions in a quiet house on a quiet street in a small regional city would constitute, for some, the very definition of sadness. Rather than deal with a world which doesn't always agree with him, he retreats to a world he can control. And there he dabbles and scribbles, brushes toast crumbs off his lap, composing half-finished essays, copying passages from books, making shorthand notes of ideas he will never realise. He is like Sterne's Uncle Toby but without the eccentric affection of family around him. He is like an aged version of Flaubert's Bouvard or Pécuchet, a dilettante of received ideas. He reads Montaigne, but he is not Montaigne, not as lucid or honest, or as self-reflective. He is sexless. He could be a bodhisattva but he tends more to the solipsistic, and often falls asleep in the very minute after one of his brightest ideas has occurred. He avoids any full-blooded engagement with life, and fails to execute his responses; and so, yes, his situation is sad, pathetic even.

But this is not FB. It is not the man I met in the bookshop, the man I lunched with, nor the author I have read. My feeling upon meeting him was that he was a man who had fully digested the *absurdity* of human endeavours, in the sense that we as humans so repeatedly get things wrong, and particularly in the sense of our habitual violence towards each other. For FB to read a writer like

Montaigne was not to luxuriate in noble ideas but to dig even deeper into that strata of absurdity. The capacity of wise men to articulate each thought, each perfectly put sentence of balance and truth, only made the behaviour of our species seem even crazier. And so the pendulum swung. The abstract versus the real. He saw it in geology, in morphology, he saw it in politics, he saw it all around him in the architecture of Geelong. A beautifully sited town, on gentle slopes falling to the curving shores of the bay, with its view of the You Yangs across the water a picturesque equivalent to Posillipo. And what had been done with such a situation? The beauty had been almost entirely obscured by rough and makeshift colonial deals and careless modern alignments.

So rather than contributing to the tragic human seesaw of beauty and wilfulness, he preferred, in the end, to say little. To live his quiet life and to stay put, even in far-from-ideal professional circumstances. For how, in a world caught inside this tragic oscillation, could he achieve anything anywhere? Surely he would only add to its absurd momentum?

This, I believe, was FB's attitude in the years just before he wrote *The Great Ocean Road: Dune Stabilisation and Other Engineering Difficulties*. It was a cast of mind triggered in him by the combination of what had happened with Mathilde and by Gibbon removing him from his work on the dunes. His *quiet*, therefore, was a predisposition, a sanctuary and, to some extent, a wisdom. He was not,

after all, as Mathilde had judged rightly, a crusader. As a
result of all he'd seen and felt in France, he'd arrived at
a logic suited to his local scene, which had in turn given
birth to a vision, and that vision, like his passion for
Mathilde, was rejected. But he did not lose the vision. It
would just have to wait, until the same winds of time that
scattered the sand up and down the coast had removed
whatever it was that stopped his vision from being clear
and obvious to others.

23

Change II

O NE DAY, NOT LONG AFTER FB HAD FINISHED ON THE dunes, he bumped into Anna Nielson outside Wolfgang Schmidt's rooms on Yarra Street. Anna was on her lunch break from her duties as Schmidt's secretary and agreed, at FB's suggestion, to take a stroll down Yarra Street to the water. FB was fully togged up that day, as was his wont, in elegant suit and tie, as he was meeting a surveyor on the foreshore to discuss some plans for new parking arrangements. But not until 2 pm. It was only 12.30 pm at the time, and so they spent a comfortable hour with each other in the sunshine, mostly laughing at how sore Anna had been after that day's work with the Croatian women, and also sharing jokes about how odd Geelong was in this, that and the other way. Like so many towns of supposedly second-rate character, Geelong often inspired this kind of self-deprecating humour in its inhabitants. It also inspired

talk of trips away, to other Australian cities, or overseas – anywhere, really, but Geelong. But as FB and Anna
strolled along Yarra Street and then along the foreshore
towards the Botanical Gardens he mentioned nothing of
his time away. In passing she casually mentioned a trip
she had once made to London, but only in passing. It was
a gentle hour, full of light touches of mirth and humour
and, from FB's account, it would be fair to say they were
shy in each other's company. They parted, agreeing that
they should do it again sometime.

In the following couple of years it was Anna who encouraged FB to sit down and write his book on the Ocean Road.
Impressed by the occasional articles he was writing on local
bridges, tunnels, aqueducts and the like, she told him she
thought he had something even better in him. Why didn't
he produce something on all the work he'd done along
the coast – which, after all, had taken him to France? He
laughed off her suggestion, it seems, or so she told me, but
quite obviously her encouragement was having its effect.

When FB took possession of the Renault Ondine they
began taking weekend drives into the landscape to look
at the early colonial bridges he was interested in. By this
time, he was already arguing for the preservation of these
bridges, often proposing to Gibbon that road alignments
be updated rather than the bridges be destroyed. FB and
Anna would picnic from the boot of the Ondine by the
Wilson iron bridge at Shelford, the Chinamans Bridge
over the Goulburn at Nagambie, and occasionally, if they

could synchronise their time off work, they would venture up into New South Wales to look at the Lennox bridges along the Hume Highway and in the wider Sydney area.

Entirely through happenstance, FB was still occasionally seconded to work along the Great Ocean Road, but not, of course, on anything to do with dunes. He worked on occasional realignment, drainage and retaining projects triggered by destructive weather. But Anna noticed that if she ever suggested that they take the Ondine for a run along the coast he would baulk at the idea. On the weekends the nose of the Renault would always be pointed inland.

Then, quite suddenly, in the autumn of 1980, FB broke off his friendship with Anna. He didn't explain his reasons other than to say he needed to be alone. He became quite brusque when Anna pressed him on it. She was understandably hurt but also began to worry. She asked Dennis Keating, a mutual friend who was also an engineer in the Geelong division of the CRB, to keep an eye on him. When Dennis Keating phoned Anna in early April to say that FB had taken two weeks off and flown to Holland, she was mystified. In their perpetual banter about 'daggy old Geelong' he'd always joked that he had no interest in overseas travel anymore and that for him a quiet life in Victoria was quite sufficient. She'd felt that beneath all the jocularity he was quite serious about this. And yet now he'd quite suddenly shot off to the Netherlands.

That winter Anna Nielson moved across town from East Geelong to Brassey Avenue in Highton. She wouldn't have said that the break with FB had anything to do with her sudden need for a move, but perhaps it did. She'd heard nothing more from Dennis Keating about FB, nothing about how his trip went or whether he had returned to work refreshed or even come back to work at all. She knew that in a town the size of Geelong it wouldn't be long before she'd bump into him, or at least sight the Ondine, but she busied herself with the new house and tried to put him out of her mind.

On a Saturday morning in late October she was at home feeling bored and tired after a long week in Schmidt's rooms when out of the corner of her eye she saw a blue flash through the window. The Ondine had pulled into her driveway.

As he got out of the car FB looked sheepish and felt sheepish, if his own words are anything to go by.

The great comfort and fun of our connection means she'll probably open the door, when I know I deserve to have it slammed shut. But all this — no, everything — is bigger than both of us. The sand must drift — so we take the longue durée *view.*

And so it was.

†

They were kindred spirits in a sleepy hollow. The population of Geelong at that time was less than a hundred and fifty-thousand people, and amongst that number there was not one other person whose companionship either of them could have enjoyed so much, or grown so fond of. They were both quiet, strong-willed people with deep interests. The ongoing stimulation of dealing with and transcribing Wolfgang Schmidt's psychoanalytic cases gave Anna a stimulating professional life without ever being able to talk about it. While she no longer played the piano seriously, as a younger woman she had graduated from the Conservatorium of Music in Melbourne, and of course FB was accomplished on the violin. They shared a quiet but jet black sense of humour, and took little interest in the football or the Grammar School, the twin obsessions of the town. They read, they liked to drive west when the wattle was out, and neither of them particularly enjoyed the stereotypical Australian summers. They had nothing against either Aboriginals or 'New Australians', and they both enjoyed chocolate, mussels from the bay, and well-bletted medlars. In short, they felt almost at home with each other.

†

As he got out of the Ondine in Brassey Avenue, FB had brought one important secret with him to help engineer his soft return. He held it under his arm as he came up the driveway.

Anna straightened her skirt and blouse and opened the

door even before he had reached it. She put her hand on her hip and glowered at him.

When she finally asked, 'Who told you where to find me?' FB could already see the amusement in her eyes. *What would her Dr Schmidt have to say about me?* he wondered.

They sat at Anna's kitchen table, FB's tweed jacket draped over a captain's chair, Anna leaning forward with her slender hands clasped on the formica. His secret lay between them, a tattered manila folder the colour of wet sand, tied up in a cross with his mother's kitchen string.

24

Dunes in Themselves

H E'D FLOWN TO AMSTERDAM, TAKEN A TRAIN SOUTH TO Middelburg in the province of Zeeland, and then a bus to the coast at Domburg. When he got off the bus the day was pale grey and still, but even without wind he could immediately smell the salt, the marram grass and the sand. He retrieved his luggage and walked the short mile along a pleasant canal to his hotel overlooking the beach. He had booked a second-floor room to make sure he had a good view of what he had come there to think about.

He was still tired from the flight, but he could not sleep, not now that he'd arrived. The room was small but comfortable, and he was happy with the view. He took a shower, smoked his first cigarette in twelve years, and then immediately ventured out onto the dunes.

Piet Mondrian was concerned with a harmony not of the human and his natural environment, but of nature

working through the senses into the human's *spiritual* environment. '*The power of the harmony inherent in existing things,*'
he wrote, '*must be attributed to the* living beauty *of nature that
acts upon* all our senses *simultaneously. For nature does not move
us through visual appearance alone.*'

That is a difficult admission for a painter to make and
one that eventually led Mondrian to abandon figurative
representation entirely in favour of his famous horizontal and vertical grids of primary colours. But it had
been the dunes, and never those colourful grids, that
had resonated with FB. It had been another comment
of Mondrian's, which had kept resonating through the
years, to such an extent that as his memories of Mathilde
and 1968 began slowly to *granulate*, to disperse into the
person he'd become, he decided to disrupt what had
become his undramatic local life and make his sudden
journey to Domburg.

'*We are no longer natural enough to be quite one with nature,*'
Mondrian had written, '*but not yet sufficiently spiritual to be
quite free of nature.*'

†

As he stepped out from the porch of the Domburg hotel
into the miraculous sea light of the Zeeland coast, FB
felt an almost overwhelming anxiety rising in his throat.
It had been with him for some months now, this feeling
of being caught between. He could barely distinguish

282

Mathilde's outline anymore, yet she remained the defining figure of his life. He had become increasingly fearful that what he had experienced with her, and through her, was slowly dwindling into the mundane. Being banned from the dunes he felt exiled from his vision, and now, as the years passed, he had begun to question whether he even cared anymore. About *anything*. About Anna, about his work, or his memories. This terrified him, and in the workaday routine of his life in Geelong he began to realise that something had to be done to stay in touch.

He could not bring himself to return to France, but lying alone in his bed one night in Milipi Avenue, he'd figured out this alternative. It didn't for one second occur to him that it was in any way *pathetic*. He would go not back to Paris, nor to La Teste-de-Buch or Cap Ferret, but to where the dunes that had brought them together in the Galerie Sarcon were painted. He had no need to see the actual paintings again, but he did now have the need to see the real things, the dunes in themselves.

Was this some predestined self-confrontation, I ask myself, or a belated pursuit for a self that was no longer singular? Was it FB himself who had become the distant figure on the flat horizon? Or was it just a middle-aged man's holiday from a life that had disappointingly slipped towards the careless and automatic?

†

He walked the dunes that first jetlagged day in Domburg, and over the three days following. He looked at the marram tufts shining sleek in the glare, and pictured his younger self standing with Mathilde in front of the Mondrian dunes in the Galerie Sarcon in the Rue des Quatre-Vents. The Enlightenment and Romantic era aristocrats had holidayed at Domburg, as they had at Arcachon, but Mondrian belonged to neither of those crowds. He was a theosophist, a kind of artist-priest, and it was in the clear atmosphere of the Zeeland coast during the summers of 1907, '08 and '09 that he began to move from what he called an 'unconscious naturalistic vision' to a 'universal' or 'pure plastic vision'. It was as if, in the unusually luminous Domburg light, he had developed X-ray vision and had begun to 'see through things', as he put it. Little by little, during those three Domburg summers, the outer recognisable form of the world began to fall away from his pictures, and it was in the very dunes where FB now walked that this had begun to happen.

The paintings FB and Mathilde had seen in Paris had certainly still been recognisable as dunes, but they also, quite literally in their infra-colour fields, resembled X-rays of the known coastal environment. For a theosophist, who aspires to a non-material life of the spirit, this perhaps could be an expected progression. But who would have imagined that it would propel Mondrian from the dunes of Zeeland to the urbanist geometric colour grids for which he has ultimately become known? Life and art are nothing if not unforeseen, and when Mondrian made the incredible claim in 1919 that 'eventually natural appearance will cease to exist', he was not referring to any generic annihilation or apocalypse to come. What was driving him on his path towards the 'pure plastic vision' that would 'see through things' was a yearning to somehow transcend or, as he said, to 'neutralise' the tragic element of life. In other words, he was trying to avoid the pain of living on earth.

As FB walked the dunes he did not walk alone. As a civil engineer he walked with the knowledge of the extraordinary feats of land reclamation that had been achieved in that part of Holland, and his mind could not help but survey the rhythm of the regular timber groynes running down from the dunes along the beach to the water, and consequently to compute accumulation and subsidence, projective wind vectors and their gradient effects, even a putative deep botanical past of the now marram-dominated hummocks. All this as he also walked as a lonely lover. Twelve years earlier in Paris, she had stood beside him in front of the paintings of the dunes, but now she was nowhere but inside him, as he stood in those dunes themselves.

Thus, if you were to paint an Australian man standing in the dunes of Domburg sometime in April 1980, you would have to paint more than just the figure in the landscape for your picture to be true.

Eventually, on that first day, he retraced his steps along the dune path and made his way back towards the town.

That night he dined in the hotel restaurant and went up early to his room. He was exhausted and washed out from the long flight and then the walk, and he slept soundly until just before the dawn, when he was woken by the sound of rain.

†

It would have come as no surprise to any of FB's engineering colleagues that he had chosen this part of the world to visit on his first overseas trip in so long. Zeeland, which translates into English as 'sea land', was home to the Deltawerken, or Delta Works, a vast post-World War II reclamation project that had barred estuaries, joined isolated islands and ultimately shortened the coastline of Holland by seven hundred kilometres. The Eastern Scheldt, a storm surge barrier across the Scheldt River, involving sixty-two sluice gates, each forty metres wide, was mid-construction at the time of FB's visit and would have been reason enough for him to visit Zeeland. But while the Deltawerken was his perfect camouflage, the Eastern Scheldt storm surge barrier was the last thing on his mind.

He walked the dunes, ate his meals either in the hotel or on the terrace of the stately Badpaviljoen, he smoked cigarettes, and he wrote in his journal. While breakfasting on the Badpaviljoen terrace on his third day in the town, he struck up conversation with an Englishman at the next table, a mathematics professor from the University of East Anglia holidaying alone after the recent death of his wife. Professor John Coulthard had made a comment in passing about FB's penchant for a breakfast cigarette, where-upon FB had promptly stubbed out his filtered Dunhill, presuming that the Englishman didn't like the smell. They got to talking then, and FB learnt that Coulthard, far from being averse to smoking, was actually attempting, in the most reserved English manner, to cadge a smoke from his neighbour. They both laughed at the misunderstanding, which then led to FB's admission that he was smoking himself for the first time in many years, simply because he was on holiday. Two Dunhills were subsequently lit and the two middle-aged men sat talking on the sunlit terrace until midday.

The next day they breakfasted together again, without being so forward as to make any formal arrangement. But FB agreed to meet John Coulthard that same afternoon on the Ooststraat, Domburg's main shopping street, to share a beer and then take a stroll along the beach.

At 4 pm they met in a small pub along the Ooststraat, a block back from the water. They sat outside under an awning, at a heavy timber outdoor dining table from where they could watch Domburgians of all ages going about their business on bicycles.

John Coulthard was tall and heavy-boned, with curly but receding salt-and-pepper hair and smooth olive skin. He had a kind smile, though one that seemed to squeeze itself up as if from a long way down in his quiet and studious personality. They shared a bowl of peanuts and resumed where they'd left off in the morning, talking about Coulthard's world at the university, also about Margaret Thatcher, Malcolm Fraser, test cricket and the Deltawerken. Before long, however – before they'd finished their first beers, in fact – John Coulthard began talking about his wife, about her slow demise from breast cancer, and eventually about how much he was struggling without her.

Coulthard's wife Fiona had been Irish, from Dublin, and they'd met when they were both undergraduates at Cambridge. 'She was the spark I needed,' Coulthard told FB. 'She was doing a history major, she was full of ideas, politically headstrong, while I was just a shy little maths guy, I suppose. God knows what she saw in me, but I couldn't really believe my good fortune. We started going out together and, well, she seemed to like me. I took her home to Norfolk to meet my parents, which I was nervous about, because she was Irish, but she charmed them as well. She was a very capable person and introduced me to pubs, to travel, to thinking seriously about where England, Ireland and the rest of Europe was going. Before that I'd not thought too much about anything but my own grades, and hockey and cricket, my own achievements.'

He paused then, closed his eyes ever so briefly and began shaking his head. 'And now, you see,' he said, looking at FB with a slightly bewildered expression, 'here I am on my own again.'

FB let John Coulthard talk. They ordered more beers and he listened as the grieving mathematician described a blissful married life, how he and Fiona both became members of the British Socialists and then the International Marxist Group, where they became friendly with Tariq Ali, amongst others. 'All this was Fiona's doing,' John Coulthard explained. 'She had a heart, you know, and it wasn't ever cancelled out by her mind or her involvement with academia. As you probably remember, the late sixties was a complicated time, both sexually and politically, not to say *philosophically*, but Fiona steered us both through all that so that even I developed a kind of certitude that really wasn't in my nature — and still isn't.'

The Coulthards had been unable to have children and, after toying with the idea of fostering and adoption, eventually decided against it. But really, John told FB, 'We were so busy that we just didn't get around to it. I wish we had now.'

He was forlorn, there was no doubt, and obviously needed to talk. The two men smoked FB's Dunhills and watched the Domburgians gliding by, as the professor of mathematics tried to find words for his despair. Strangely, FB, who aside from the death of his own parents had had little experience of grief, didn't feel uncomfortable or even inadequate as he sat and listened to the grieving Englishman. Occasionally he would laugh with Coulthard as he recalled anecdotes from his and Fiona's years together, and when Coulthard grew increasingly inconsolable and explained how marooned he felt there on the Dutch coast without her, the tears in the Englishman's eyes, rather than alarming FB or making him nervous, only brought tears to his own.

John Coulthard obviously sensed the undivided nature of FB's presence across the table, his readiness to listen to and even understand the sorrows of a stranger. More than once, in the course of that three hours they spent together under the pub awning, he thanked FB and apologised for the imposition. But the apology was only offered out of habit. At a more profound and specific level, he could sense that having the opportunity to talk to a sympathetic and intelligent stranger was more than luck. It felt as natural as it was necessary and, as he described Fiona's last difficult weeks, first in the hospital at Norwich and then at home with John and her sister Mary, who was a nurse and had travelled across from Liverpool to help, his tears began to flow freely.

FB took no fright at the grown man crying across the table from him. He reassured Coulthard, suggesting that his wife did in fact still live in his life, by her example, in the memories he had of their life together, and the way she went about things. These simply expressed realities seemed to help the mathematician, whom FB felt was suffering almost as much from self-doubt as from the loss of his wife. It was as if the Englishman wanted to return to shore but had lost his navigator. The idea that perhaps, despite her physical passing, Fiona's spirit was still there with him, as a support and guide, seemed to make some sense. FB saw the flicker of relief in his eyes.

They said their goodbyes just before 7 pm, after Coulthard's catharsis had seemed to complete itself and the talk had turned back to the Deltawerken. As they rose, John Coulthard once again apologised for his upwellings and FB told him, with a smile, to 'cut it out'. Perhaps they would see each other on the terrace of the Badpaviljoen in the morning. John Coulthard said he hoped so, before saying good evening and walking off in the direction of the canal.

Back in his hotel room, FB sat in front of the window looking out over the dunes onto the water. The sky was almost colourless over the blue ink of the sea. It had been an unusually intense meeting, but he was in no way exhausted or regretful of what had happened. On the contrary, he felt unusually contented and within half an hour he had pulled his chair up to the small painted wooden desk below the window and started to write.

†

What he couldn't recall in that room overlooking the North Sea in Domburg, he researched and rediscovered on his return to Australia. But he was surprised at what he could remember, and what he did know, from all the years of working on, and thinking about, that strip of sandy and sheer coast where he grew up and along which a few bright men with a sense of practical civic duty and a taste for development had decided there should be a road.

He sat in that window of luminous Domburg light for ten days and put down in writing what he could. There was no mention of Paris, only brief mentions of Arcachon and the Gascony coast, and certainly no mention of opening the door of a canary's cage and wondering what would happen next. But it was all in there, like a deep moonless night under the daylights of the world. What it was about his interaction with John Coulthard that suddenly cleared the path for him to begin writing the book is hard to say. Perhaps it was as simple, and as *Catholic*, as him realising that his own loss could be much worse. What if, for instance, Mathilde had not put her political and philosophical ideals above her feelings for him, and they had married and settled on the Bassin d'Arcachon, only for her to die before her time?

To think that the slim history I found so compelling when I was making my songs about the Great Ocean Road was begun, if not wholly written, on the faraway coast of Zeeland, seems plausible to me now. And to think further on how this came to be so, to think about the stories in our hearts and how slowly they travel, is really no different from thinking about sand. Sand that is the most consumed resource in the world after freshwater and air. Sand that makes a grain out of a mountain and a mountain out of grains. Sand that has no passport, and no conventions or manners, except to change, to change again, to keep moving always and to always change. Sand that has no beginning and no end.

25

Accumulation

I N 1983 THE COUNTRY ROADS BOARD CEASED TO
exist – or, rather, was subsumed into a body calling
itself the Road Construction Authority. Alwyn Gibbon
took this moment as his cue to retire as divisional
engineer in Geelong. He had been in the chair for
almost the entirety of FB Herschell's career and one
could be forgiven for expecting FB to feel a certain yet
somehow indefinite sense of *aeration* at the prospect of his
forthcoming departure. But it seems things were not that
simple. He had self-published *The Great Ocean Road: Dune
Stabilisation and Other Engineering Difficulties* in 1982, with a
dedication to Anna Nielson and a quote from Camus on
the opening page. The book took up its place on municipal
and university library shelves, and on the shelves of some
of his engineering colleagues and correspondents, but
apart from that was summarily ignored. It is these days

virtually impossible to find. FB did, however, send a copy to Professor Lacombe in Paris, who had himself only recently retired from academic life to devote his time to writing. Professor Lacombe wrote a very enthusiastic letter in return, in which he acknowledged, for the first time, how difficult things must have been for FB while he was in France, and how impressive it was therefore to observe how he had '*adapted the primitive certainties of the Revolutionary era to the intricacies of the Australian environment. To encase those lessons in a work of wider social history involving the war recovery project that was the construction of the Great Ocean Road shows the innate subtlety of your intelligence, which of course you did not need to come to Paris to learn.*'

FB also received a letter from one Mrs N. Considine of Wishart Street, Port Fairy, who fondly recalled the day in 1965 when she and her husband Pat, who at the time was divisional engineer for the Warrnambool district, enjoyed a round of golf with FB on the links at Port Fairy. '*Do you remember that visit, Mr Herschell?*' she wrote. '*I for one remember you as handsome young Frank and I also remember a little conversation we had about France and the dunes. As a result, I enjoyed your erudite book on the Ocean Road immensely.*'

The publication of the book had once again attracted the attention of head engineers in the Melbourne office who, in the midst of plans for the restructuring of the department, began to consider FB not as Gibbon's direct replacement – for there would be no such replacement in the new Road Construction Authority – but as a candidate for the correspondingly senior role in the Geelong and wider Barwon area. FB was called one day to a friendly meeting over lunch and sounded out about his attitude to such an arrangement. According to Anna Nielson, he was flattered, and he even spoke to her about potential projects, including the phasing out of *Ammophila arenaria*, which may finally have a chance to fly.

Three months later, after a curious silence from Melbourne, which FB put down to the vagaries of the kind of centralised bureaucracy he had read about in the novels of Kafka, the senior positions of the new authority were announced. He, like Kafka, was not on the list. No explanation was given, no apology offered, and thus any prospect of FB returning to his main vocational pathway was over. In Victoria, marram grass, like asbestos, was still perceived as a key ingredient of the state's apparatus, which was well evidenced in the ensuing months and years when, in response to the severe bushfires of 16 February 1983, or Ash Wednesday as it has become known, the planting of marram grass was ramped up and redoubled all along the fire-affected littoral.

I often wonder what I would have asked FB Herschell about first, when I sat opposite him at the wool-classing table in the cafe in James Street, if I'd known then what I know now. Would I have asked about environmental weeds, unrequited love, or how to write so well about one thing when you're actually writing about another? Curiously, I find myself also thinking about the existence of God when

I think about FB Herschell. I can only put this down to the fact that so much of what I admire in him went unnoticed or unseen in this world. He is far from being a martyr in my mind, but when I think about all the programs these days to remove the marram grass and other exotic vegetation in our area, to restore our coastlines to something better resembling a balance between nature and culture, I can't help but feel melancholy on his behalf.

He must have watched that slow progression in the decades after his return from Domburg and felt a mixture of emotions. He continued with the work required of him by the new Road Construction Authority (which in 1989 morphed again into the Roads Corporation and subsequently became known as VicRoads) without once being asked to contribute the expertise that was so evident in his book. Slowly, as the 1990s approached the millennium, the rusty wheels of the governing bodies turned towards unavoidable ecological imperatives, just as Australians of all ethnic backgrounds came ever so slowly to understand what Aboriginal people had always been trying to tell them about the delicate beauty of the soils, rocks and sands of antiquity in which they lived. When the shires along the Victorian west coast, and even VicRoads itself, began commissioning detailed environmental studies prior to installing new infrastructure, FB would occasionally send laconic, dry-humoured or positively caustic letters, in which he'd annotate the increasingly corporatised double-speak, thereby pointing out the relative inconsistencies and often shallow intent of the newly fashionable meas-ures being recommended. I have read over some of these letters of annotation in the Correspondence file of his archive, and caught a new happiness in his tone. But would I really call it happiness? Is that the right word? Or is it actually a new and improved version of the *insouciance* displayed by Danny the Red and the other students in Paris in 1968, and which FB himself displayed to Gibbon when he submitted his report in French? There is a sense of confidence in these letters, even of certainty, both in his own hard-won experience with dunes and in the fact that even as we attempt to rectify our old mistakes we are destined to make new ones.

I remember then that shining in his eyes when he would come into the bookshop, the flesh-and-blood man and not just his words. There we'd stand, amongst the greatest thinkers and artists, scientists and poets in the history of the world, amidst thousands of bound reckonings – yet it was still the same wonky old world. You could see it in his eyes, it was always there: all the beauty, the wisdom, and our perpetual inability to attain it.

Whenever Anna Nielson speaks to me of FB these days, she does so with a smile. Even in the weeks immediately after his death, when the memory of his demise in the hospital must have been fresh, and the loss of his compan-ionship palpable, she would grin at the mention of his name. I take this as a great tonic proof against his life being viewed as a failure, or somehow unfulfilled. He lives on not only in his book and in the papers of his archive but in the spirit of his best friend's recollection.

†

It was during those weeks immediately after his death that Anna offered to show me through FB's house. She was concerned, she said, about what would and wouldn't be noticed by the book auctioneers, the antique dealers, even the people from St Vincent de Paul. 'Plus,' she said, with her own twinkle in the eye, 'you might just enjoy having a look around.'

When I arrived at the house on a sweltering hot day the following week, the first thing I noticed, apart from the complete ordinariness of the treeless working-class street, was the absence of the Renault Ondine. It wasn't in the garage and it wasn't parked out the front. So where was it? I felt almost as if the stylish car had, along with its driver, gone to its own stylish afterlife. Subsequently I learnt that I was right about this – the Ondine had been bought by a retired female High Court judge, who lived on the Yarra River in Melbourne and was on the board of the ANZ Bank, the Victorian Racing Club, the Alliance Française and also the steering committee of Melbourne's annual French Film Festival. She had known FB through the Alliance Française, where from time to time through the years he attended classes. At his encouragement, she was apparently spending her retirement years attempting to translate *La Littérature à l'estomac*, the seminal 1951 essay by perhaps FB's favourite of all French authors, Julien Gracq.

The second thing that struck me about my visit to the house in Milipi Avenue was the single bed. In a house bursting at the seams with books both old and new, FB's original bed, where he had slept both as a child and as an old man, remained wedged into the shadowy corner of his bedroom. It was the constancy of the scene that struck me. The man of sand, who first worked to keep it in its place and then to understand the deeper logic behind its natural propensity to drift and shift about, had stayed put himself for the long duration of his life. The infant, the boy, the young musician, the brilliant engineer with international horizons, the writer, the man of quiet defeat and a broken heart, the jocular interloper, the reader, the regretter, the scholar, the sage, all those facets of him had shifted, interchanged, subsided, slackened, heaped up and stabilised themselves in that one small room. Once the Ondine was parked of an evening, once the fish or steak or quiche was eaten and the current book was read, this was where he'd survey his feeling heart and thinking head. This was his Wenceslas Square, his Eccles Street, his Pequod. His workstation and dreamhouse.

I stood for some time alone in that room, a little confused and unable to comprehend the feeling that he was only partially absent. I felt like an intruder, almost an idolater in a sacred space, staring at his green pillow, his tartan blankets, the built-in shelving still full of papers and notebooks, his little desk with scratchings in the timber he most probably made when he was a child. It was not the room of a famous man, a man for whom everything he had to offer found its rightful and grateful recipients, but nevertheless I had the strong sense as I stood there that the living FB Herschell, the man who had dwelt and dreamed in this room, the man who had lain awake, laughed, and listened to the birds at dawn, was at that very moment being transferred into a character of my imagination. Had death stripped him of any control of his future destiny, just as it had made space for such a deep and abiding resonance? As I stepped between the desk and bed to peer at the contents of his shelves, I sensed again the voiding of space behind me that I had felt by the river when I had first learnt of his death. This time, though, the voiding was not in the shape of a lizard's tail but seemed instead a bigger, wider, more open form of light. Conscious of this change, I felt then that I was standing on the shore between a life and whatever came after it. Everything was mixed, there was no division, no beginning or end.

When the moment passed I was left again with the ordinary furniture of his room. I had a sudden desire – no, a *need* – to find out more. I knew then that I would somehow bear testimony, as much to the beautiful quality of solitude I felt in that room as to the man who had lived there.

Anna had left me alone in the bedroom but now, quietly

overwhelmed, I re-emerged to greet her in the hallway. She showed me through the other rooms, into the galley kitchen, down the hallway to the little back porch and through an idiosyncratic old screen door to the garden. The garden was the only space that was not full of pages. Instead: a white Geelong sky, a bare patch of sunburnt lawn, a birdbath. We stood in silence for a time looking at that birdbath before turning and going back inside.

Despite the treasure trove of knowledge the house contained – the first editions, the rare ephemera, not to mention the extensive cache of musical scores – there was only one book I was really interested in that day. I had hoped that perhaps there might be a few copies left over, multiple copies, in a box somewhere, perhaps even under that single bed. But no, he had only ever kept one copy, Anna said, and she assured me it had already been taken away amongst six boxes of especially valuable material by Australian Book Auctions, who had come through the previous week. There were three piles of books still on the living room floor, set aside for the auctioneers to pick up on their final visit the next day, but *The Great Ocean Road: Dune Stabilisation and Other Engineering Difficulties* was not amongst them.

I left Milipi Avenue in the early afternoon, sweaty and moved. All the subtlety, all the deep feeling and close attention I had sensed in his book on the Ocean Road, was somehow contained in that house. His papers were to be collected, an archive was apparently going to be assembled at the university, and I resolved to investigate that when it became available. I also resolved to find my way to the auction of FB's books when it came up in Melbourne. I had a little money set aside, and now I knew what for. There was that one book, which in the early years of this century had been a portal for me into a whole other way of seeing and writing about the world. It was only one book, a slim self-published volume from a quiet life, in which nearly all the most important things had been left unsaid.